5

DECEASED AND DESIST (BOOK 5)

A Harley and Davidson Mystery

LILIANA HART
LOUIS SCOTT

7th Press

To our kids -
You're worth it.

The Harley and Davidson Mystery Series

Chapter One

AGATHA HARLEY LOUNGED BACK on the couch in her war room and studied Hank. He'd changed in the year she'd known him. The tight lines around his eyes and mouth had relaxed with retirement, and he looked content. The scar across his nose only added to the mystique that was Hank Davidson.

"You know, that scar across your nose really gives you some character," she said.

"You saying I had no character before that outlaw clocked me in the face with his sawed-off?"

Agatha chuckled. "Oh, no, honey. You're full of character."

There was an ease sitting with Hank, listening to the rhythm of an afternoon April shower. Agatha pulled her socked feet onto the couch and tucked them beneath her. Hank stretched his long legs across the refurbished wooden floor until his feet rested beneath the glass coffee table.

"You've been kind of quiet about it," Hank said, "but are you doing okay with how things went down with the Rattlers last month?"

"My heart says yes, but my head still gets trapped in the reality of seeing violence and death meted out so effortlessly. I guess writing about it and witnessing the end results of it have given me a hard edge. But actually being in the middle of it is a whole other issue."

"I can understand that. The differences between theory and reality."

Agatha twisted so she directly faced him and set her hands on his thigh. Agatha felt the heaviness in her chest and still debated whether or not to bring up something that had been bothering her

"Can I ask you something?"

"Sure," he said. "As long as I don't have to promise to answer."

"I don't want to intrude, but I have to be honest." She'd not slept well the last month, and unless she wanted to spend the next year a complete zombie, she needed to open up to Hank about her struggles.

Hank placed his hand on top of hers. "Being honest is a good start. And I was only kidding about not answering. Ask me what you need to."

"I'm having a lot of trouble with the idea of us," she blurted out.

"Oh?" Hank asked.

"I mean, ever since I saw you shoot those two bikers, I've not been able to stop thinking about it. And then I saw the ease at which you dropped Skinner, and it began to scare me a little."

"I'm sorry you had to see it at all. It's a dirty business, but I've been the garbage man for decades. Our job is to do the things that others won't or can't. It's not always an easy choice."

"I understand that," she said. "But trash men don't wallow in the junk." She could feel the emotion start to bubble in her chest.

"Wow, that's pretty insulting," he said, sitting up a little. "You think I enjoy the violence?"

She chewed on her bottom lip and thought about the answer. "I don't think you hate it. I could see into your soul when Tony Smith held that gun in your face. You didn't care one way or the other if he pulled the trigger. How am I supposed to consider having a future with someone like that?" Tears trickled down her cheeks.

Hank pushed up from the couch and paced across the living room. He opened his mouth to say something, but closed it again.

"I, umm," Hank said, trying to reply.

"I'm sorry, Hank."

He nodded and grabbed the keys to his house from the antique table, and shoved through the front door without saying goodbye.

Agatha curled up on the couch until the shadows of the late afternoon encroached upon her back porch. She didn't mean for it to come out that way, but she'd expected Hank to respond differently. Honestly, she wasn't sure how the words were going to come out, but once it began to flow, she couldn't stop herself.

It was harsh and disrespectful to a man who had only lived his life to serve others.

She fumbled in the dimly lit living room to find her vibrating cell phone. Her heart began to pound. Maybe it was Hank. Maybe they could patch things up before it stewed any longer. She found the phone in between two overstuffed pillows.

"Hello," she said.

"Hey, girl. What's going down at the Harley household?"

"Heather?"

"Yep, I'm back."

"I didn't know you were gone," Agatha said, distracted.

"Funny," she said. "I've been a bit busy, but that isn't what's important. Did you and Hank have a fight? I saw him leaving your house mad as a cat that's been thrown in bathwater."

"Not now, Heather," Agatha said, rubbing her temples. "Can I call you back?"

"No way, sister. I know this game. You have no plan to call me back, and I'm dying to know what's going on with my favorite power couple."

Agatha wiped a tear that managed to roll about half way down her cheek. She wasn't going to fall apart over this man. She'd suffered through enough of Heather's dramatic moments to understand what an exercise in futility it was to vent.

"Thanks, but I just can't today. It was just a misunderstanding."

"Liar," Heather said. "But if you want to talk about it I'll be at the Taco and Waffle. I've heard Penny's working there on Sunday nights and she likes to slip free drinks in with food orders."

Agatha rolled her eyes.

"Then I'm definitely not going. I've had my fill of Penny and her snooping into my business."

"Between you and me, I heard she was hustling up to make cash to buy a place once her boyfriend returns home from the Army."

"Boyfriend?" Agatha asked.

"Word is, she met a special forces soldier who's still

fighting in the Middle East. They met on the internet, but she's head over heals in love with her war hero. Don't know where he's from. But, he's agreed to move to Rusty Gun to be with her."

"Interesting."

"Looks like your Hammerin' Hank Davidson isn't going to be the only out-of-town hero living here."

"Maybe so. You know, Penny did ask me about buying or renting my house. I thought she was just being nosy. Who knows? Maybe she has found someone. Good for her."

"So, are you up to knocking a few back?" Heather asked. "I've got some juicy news to share."

Agatha sat up from the couch. It wasn't seven o'clock yet and she hadn't eaten since she and Hank grilled burgers at lunch. Against her better judgment, she agreed to go.

"Okay, but just for a little while. Come pick me up," Agatha said.

"I'm in your driveway."

Agatha blew out a breath. "That's kind of creepy. Give me five."

She dropped back on the couch, already wishing she could cancel, but Heather was relentless. She'd come in and drag her out by the hair if necessary. She groaned and got up from the couch, and her phone vibrated again.

"I said give me five minutes," she said.

The line was quiet.

"Hello?" she asked.

No one answered, although she knew the line was connected. She listened for sound—breathing or evidence of a prank call—or maybe Hank still too upset to speak. Her call display showed an unknown caller signal.

"Okay, last chance," she said. "Hello."

Still nothing. Agatha looked at the phone and wondered why she was being so patient. It wasn't like she received a ton of calls. Maybe that was it. The few calls she did get were from people she knew very well. Maybe one of them was in need. Or maybe there was another explanation.

Her finger shook as she aimed for the End Call button. What if? What if it was him again? It had been over fifteen years since he'd been sent to prison. Would he be able to find her? What would he do if he did? The possibilities sent a cold frisson of fear down her spine.

Chapter Two

EARLY APRIL WAS a beautiful time in central Texas. There were the typical rainy days, but it was nothing like the seasonal whims of Philadelphia. There were years when snow still covered the ground this time of year back home. Hank never thought he'd love to live anyplace but home, but he loved it here.

He couldn't leave the motorcycle sitting in the garage on such a perfect day, so he cranked it up and headed off to visit Sully just outside of Waxahachie. The former outlaw was still convalescing at a cousin's trailer, and Hank was concerned his injuries from the beating he'd received needed medical attention.

Hank also needed the saddle time to clear his thoughts about the conversation he and Agatha had the day before. He regretted walking out in anger. After he'd had the day to think through his actions, he realized he responded not in anger—well, maybe a little--but mostly because what she'd said hurt.

Hank had accepted killing as a reality of his job. There were many occasions where it was kill or be killed. It was the very nature of the sort of criminals he hunted. The very worst of the worst serial killers who devalued the price of life as a simple means to satisfying their fix for death. There were only two ways out of a situation like that—capture them or kill them.

In hindsight, maybe there was a satisfaction in saving the taxpayers millions of dollars in incarceration, court, and appeals processes. But the truth was, Hank only killed when it was a matter of life or death. What he'd done to the outlaws that night was completely different. His and Agatha's lives were on the line, and if he hadn't shown himself as top dog, they'd both be dead. Shooting those bikers with non-mortal wounds had gotten his point across.

He remained haunted by the night his wife, Tammy, had been killed by The Bonekeeper. Hank felt deeply responsible for trying to take the notorious serial killer into custody with just the two of them. She'd been a great cop, but they hadn't been enough. And it had cost her life. Hank never considered whether The Bonekeeper would have complied with surrender and arrest. Instead, Hank strangled him until he knew for sure the murderer was dead.

Never once had he thought about handling the situation differently. The killer killed, so he was killed. But, was that Hank's duty to serve as judge, jury and executioner? Agatha's words stung. Not because they weren't true, but possibly because they were the truth.

Sure, Ratchet held him at bay with a double-barrel sawed-off shotgun, but Butcher was only armed with a club. Did he really have to be shot, even if it was in the foot?

Hank shook his head to dismiss the thoughts. He still carried the bruises and stitches from the attack that night behind Reverend Graham's Harley Davidson shop. The pain was a stark reminder that there was evil in the world —and yes, they'd deserved what they'd gotten.

Hank down shifted the motorcycle as he entered the town limits of Rusty Gun. He spotted Deputy Karl Johnson walking across the street toward his mom's restaurant, Bucky's Brisket Basket.

Karl waved and waited for him on the sidewalk, so Hank pulled into a parking spot and cut the engine.

"Hey, man," Hank said. "Big surprise seeing you here. I didn't think your mom opened this early."

"She doesn't, but mama said Penny's had the brisket on the smoker all day, and it was okay to come over and grab a plate before I go on duty. Why don't you join me? I hate eating alone."

Hank's mouth watered. He'd never tasted better than Sheila Johnson's brisket. She said the secret was in the dry rub she used.

"You are one lucky fella," Hank said. "You've got a great mom. I hope you let her know that."

"She's the best," Karl said. "It's always been just me and her. She worked like a dog after my daddy left, and I never wanted for anything. I always thought she might find somebody to settle down with, but she said she's married to the restaurant and that's more than enough. Personally, I think things were so bad with my dad she probably never wants to deal with it again. I can't say I blame her. I'm glad I have very few memories of him."

"Moms are special," Hank said. "They love us no matter what."

Karl laughed. "That's the truth, but I think she might be a little fed up with her baby boy right now."

Hank frowned. He didn't like getting into anyone's business, but Karl and Sheila were both his friends. "I'm sorry. I hope it's nothing serious."

Karl sighed. "I'm kinda embarrassed to say." Karl shoved his hands into the pockets of his khaki deputy's uniform.

"Son, I'm not here to judge you. I'm your friend, but I also respect your privacy."

"Mama found out that I was messing around with someone, and she's not happy about it. At all."

"That's tough. But you're an adult, and I know you love your mom, but you're a man now. She's just trying to protect you, but ultimately what you do and who you do it with is your choice to make."

"It's Heather Cartwright," Karl said.

"In that case, I completely agree with your mom," Hank said. "Boy, are you crazy? That woman will chew you up and spit you out."

Karl looked dejected, and Hank couldn't help but laugh. He squeezed Karl's shoulder in support.

"You're not telling me anything I don't know deep down," Karl said. "I was just hoping you'd agree with me. I know I should've avoided her."

"Look, what I said still stands. It is your choice, but while you are free to jump out of a plane without a parachute, you should still think about the consequences before you leap. And if you do still chose to jump, know that those who love you will continue to love you whether you end up in the hospital or the grave."

"I guess mama was right," Karl said. "Heather is the devil."

Hank couldn't help but laugh again. "Your mother is very intuitive."

"I hate this town," Karl said, his frustration evident. "There just aren't many people like me."

"Black?"

"No," Karl said. "I don't care about that. I mean young."

"What about Penny?"

Karl rolled his eyes. "She's nuts, but even she's got a man. He's some kind of military special forces dude who's coming to live with her. I think they met on the Internet. I mean, come on. Even Penny can find love."

"Well, I'm not sure that's considered love, but who knows," Hank said. "I just hope she got that smoker ready so we can grab a few slices of brisket. It's got my mouth watering."

He slapped Karl on the back as they moved toward the restaurant's door.

"Thanks for the advice," Karl said.

"Any time. And I mean that. Besides, you gave me a good laugh. I needed one."

Karl's lips twitched.

Hank had needed the laugh. The situation with Agatha had really gotten him down. He'd checked his cell phone numerous times, but knew her well enough to know she wasn't the text and make up kind of girl.

Karl had a key to the restaurant and unlocked it. When he opened it the most wonderful smell assaulted his senses. As soon as they were inside Karl locked it again.

"Penny," Karl called out. "It's Karl, and I've got Hank with me. Just grabbing a quick plate before shift."

Hank walked over to the counter and sat on a stool. He grabbed a napkin from the metal napkin holder and wiped a bit of road grime from his face.

"Three pointer," he said, tossing the wadded up napkin in a perfect arc toward the trashcan. It hit the rim and then bounced off onto the floor.

"You better pick that up, man. My mama will skin you," Karl said, teasing.

"Your mama will skin Penny if she's left this meat smoker unattended. Where is that girl?"

Karl looked back in the kitchen, and then looked back at Hank through the server's window and shrugged.

"Penny, you here?" Karl asked, growing impatient.

"Maybe she's in the bathroom," Hank said.

"Nope, it's empty. I told mama not to hire her, but she always sees the good in others."

"Maybe her new man came to town early. I've never seen Penny not show up for work. She's nuts, but she works hard."

Hank went around the counter to grab the napkin that had fallen on the floor. It had bounced beneath the sink, but he knew how meticulous Sheila was about her restaurant being spotless, so he knelt down to get it. He saw something dark and wet on the floor, probably barbecue sauce, and he used the napkin to clean it up. But when he looked at the napkin it wasn't barbecue sauce. It was bright crimson. And fresh

"I think we might have a problem here," he called out to Karl.

"I think we do," Karl said. "Penny's dead."

Chapter Three

HANK STOOD inside the restaurant and watched as Karl strung police caution tape around the outside. He knew by Karl's response that Penny was the first dead body he'd ever seen. It wasn't like murder was an everyday occurrence in Rusty Gun.

Sheriff Reggie Coil stood outside, and Hank could tell Karl was doing his best to brief him on what they'd discovered. He also knew Coil cared about his team, and was giving Karl the one-on-one to process the trauma. It was better to talk it through than to allow it to stew in your head for too long. Unaddressed thoughts could become toxic.

Hank had guided Karl in securing the crime scene until Coil arrived. Coil had just returned from Austin where he'd had his final deposition from the state's law enforcement ethics commission.

During the case last month where Coil's former partner, Tony Smith, aka Axle, tried killing him and his family for a long-lost treasure, it was discovered that Coil had purposefully kept quiet about two murders in which Smith had confessed to him. As part of Smith's plan to control Coil, he'd backed him into an ethical corner by only telling him enough to suspect there were murders, but not enough to corroborate the information.

Hank unlocked the doors for Coil and let him inside. Karl chose to stay outside and keep the curious away.

"Can I ask how it went?" Hank asked.

Coil walked past him to get beyond the big, glass windows and the dozen or so curious onlookers.

"Well, I'm here aren't I?"

Hank wanted to congratulate him, but Coil didn't seem as excited as he should be. "They made the right call. I'm just glad you can put it behind you."

"Well, it isn't totally behind me. The ethics commission has placed me on a one year probation. I gotta take a few executive management courses out of Dallas."

"That's not too bad. You like Dallas."

"And, they've referred my case over to the State Attorney General to review for prosecution."

"Whoa," Hank said. No wonder Coil didn't look like he'd received good news. "Ava Grace O'Brien?"

"Yep."

Ava Grace O'Brien was a no-nonsense corruption fighter who never apologized for bringing the corrupt ones to justice. No matter how powerful they were. Of course, that had made her lots of enemies, but the public loved her. And there was nothing she liked better than putting away dirty cops.

When Hank had been stuck between a rock and a hard place with the Texas Rangers, Agatha had given him Ava's contact information in case he needed an attorney. He'd found out later that Agatha and Ava had been roommates at TCU. Hank had once threatened to turn Coil over to her if he didn't come clean about the gold and the Lone

Star Rattlers outlaw motorcycle club. But he only had access to O'Brien through Agatha. It was an ace-in-the-hole that might be needed.

"It'll be okay," Coil said, but he didn't seem too convinced. "Seems every witness but me is either dead or an outlaw."

"Then how about we solve this case to take your mind off it. I'm sure y'all don't get fresh murders everyday around here. She was Karl's first body."

"He tried briefing me outside, but he was too shaken up. He'll make for a great deputy one day, but today's not that day."

He and Coil had been through violent deaths enough to know how to cope. Cops either got through it with gallows humor or just by shutting everything off and becoming numb. Hank had never worked a murder with Coil, but the cold, empty look in his eyes showed there was no humor in his defenses.

"Run it down for me," Coil said. He stood in the middle of the restaurant, hands on hips, soaking in the scene.

"According to Sheila, Penny came in about six this morning to get the meat on the smoker so it'd be ready by supper. Once she did that she went to work the morning shift at the café, and she was back here by ten o'clock or so. I was heading back into town after a ride and saw Karl as I rode through.

"He said Sheila told him it was okay to grab a plate of brisket before he started his shift, and he invited me to join him. That was around three o'clock. Karl unlocked the front door and we came in. He called out for Penny, but she didn't answer."

"You sure he had to unlock the door?" Coil asked.

"Yeah, he unlocked the door. And then he locked it

behind us." Hank realized he was more a witness right now than a cop.

"Which means Penny knew whoever it was because she let them in and then locked the door behind her."

"Possibly," Hank said. "Or maybe they've been hiding out since last night."

"You ever in here when Sheila locks up?" Coil asked.

Hank thought about it. Sheila was thorough. She'd have known if someone was in her place. "I guess you're right. Okay, so Penny knows her killer and unlocks the door to let them in. The body is in the walk-in cooler."

"I don't want to see her right now. I'd like to get a feel for how things played out before getting involved in the evidence."

"It's okay to call her by name," Hank said, a little aggravated at Coil's attitude. "Calling her evidence doesn't mean you're not going to recognize her when we walk in there."

"Right now, Hank, that body in there is evidence."

"One thing I learned after almost three decades on the job and enough dead bodies to drown in was that there's always room for compassion. Whether you know the victim or not. It's what allows us to keep our humanity."

Coil took a step closer to Hank, and Hank glowered down at him. He wouldn't be intimidated by the likes of Coil. Friend or not.

"Or maybe compassion is a weakness that drove you away from the job. I can't afford to get emotional about this. I'm sorry if I won't shed tears today, but the best thing I can do for her is to keep my feelings in check until we catch the SOB who killed her."

Hank wasn't sure how to respond to that. It was true, every word of it was true, but it didn't mean he agreed with it. If he was going to work side-by-side with Coil on this case, he'd have to reconcile the differences in their approach. What Hank knew they did agree on was that whoever killed Penny was skilled at the art of killing.

"I guess I wrongly assumed we were working this case together, but I see I'm no more than a witness to the crime."

Coil turned away. His gaze lingered toward the rear of the restaurant where he was told Penny's body lay. Rusty Gun was a small town, and Hank knew everyone was either connected by blood or friendship.

Hank locked his hands behind his back and recited the rest of his witness testimony. "Like I said before, Penny didn't respond when we called out. I tossed a napkin toward the garbage can but it hit the rim and fell to the floor. When I walked around behind the counter to throw it away, I noticed something on the floor. When I wiped it up with the napkin I could see it was blood. Karl had found Penny at that point and called out to me.

"We drew our weapons and cleared the rest of the building. We didn't touch or disturb anything, other than the blood I cleaned up. And Karl checked for Penny's pulse. We secured the scene and waited for you to arrive."

Coil tugged a pair of plastic hospital gloves over his large, calloused hands, "Sorry for jumping on you. I guess I'm upset knowing that O'Brien is looking over my case. I've known people she's gone after just to make a name for herself. It didn't matter if guilty or not, what people notice are the headlines. It can kill a sheriff like me to be dragged through the media. I've got an election next year."

"I can't imagine. I've never been an elected official but I know what it's like to be crucified by the media. Best advice I can give you is to say nothing beyond it being an active situation and your attorney has told you not to comment."

"Understood," Coil said. "Let's go see Penny."

Coil handed Hank a pair of booties to slip over his boots. They helped prevent crime scene contamination and possibly destroying shoe print evidence. They were also very handy for keeping your own shoes clean and not carrying anything from the scene back into your own home.

The cooler door was still open, just like Karl had found it. The six-by-eight-foot galvanized steel container was created for maintaining items at a constant and steady state of storage.

Hank checked the external thermometer to see that the temperature had remained at the optimum for meat storage at thirty-eight degrees. A vapor proof light allowed them to see the cooler's contents clearly. Penny's body was purposefully posed in the far corner.

If Hank hadn't checked earlier, it might've appeared that Penny was just taking a nap on a stack of vegetable boxes. But, once they moved closer, it was clear that a razor-sharp blade had been cleanly pulled across her throat.

Coil switched on his flashlight to get a closer look. She'd been cleaned up after her death, but it didn't look like she put up a struggle. He moved within inches of Penny's right shoulder.

"Look at that," Hank said. "Looks like a branding."

"What do you mean?" Coil moved in to take a closer look.

"A lot of times killers, especially serial killers, like to mark their property or take a trophy. This is an impersonal space, so it's unlikely he took a souvenir from here. But he left his mark."

"He?" Coil asked.

"I'm just offering a theory," Hank said cautiously as to

not step on Coil's official toes. "But Penny unlocked the door for someone she knew. She also allowed someone to come up very close behind her. That's an act of intimacy and trust. I've not known or heard Penny was into women, so I would assume it was a man. And there's been talk around town that she's involved with some guy she met online."

"We'll wait for autopsy but COD looks pretty cut and dried. The slice runs from her left side and turns up as it fades out on the right side of her throat. Indicates that the killer was taller than she was and right handed."

Hank imitated the slicing gesture. "Or that Penny was on her knees and the killer stood above her."

"Good point," Coil said. "I've got Lieutenant Maria Rodriguez coming from home to photograph and begin processing the crime scene. Also, the county coroner is coming to claim the body."

"Does Rodriguez need any help?" Hank offered.

"No, thanks. I sent her to a crime scene investigations class at the Garland Police Department. There was a senior CSI I knew there that said she was a natural. I told Jim that he'd better not dare try to steal her away from my office."

"You think Karl will be okay?" Hank asked

"Yep. He'll help Maria. Keeping busy will be good for him, and it'll give him some much needed reality. He'll be better for the experience."

"Mind if I snap a picture of that marking on her shoulder?" Hank asked. "I want to compare it to past cases where brandings were left."

"Sure," Coil said. "She's all yours. And I mean that literally. If I get suspended pending the outcome of an investigation, I've appointed you as the interim sheriff."

"What?" Hank asked.

"I could've sworn I told you," he said, grinning.

"Nope, but you'd sure better keep yourself unsuspended. I'm retired."

"Yeah," Coil said, eyeing Hank crouched over the body. "I can see that."

Chapter Four

AT MIDNIGHT, the sheriff's office was still bursting with activity. Coil had called deputies in from surrounding counties to help solve the case. Hank remembered this part of the job. The constant push and surge of energy to track a killer. At least until you dropped from exhaustion, and he was exhausted. He and Coil had met with Penny's family earlier to deliver the official death notification.

"We're going to have to call it a night," Coil said.

"Is there anything new?" Lieutenant Rodriguez asked. She'd spent the day at the state crime lab to submit the very little physical evidence recovered from the scene. It was one of the cleanest things she'd ever processed.

Coil walked over to a wall-length dry erase board. "Not really, but we have eliminated a few angles. The blood on the napkin did indeed belong to Penny. The coroner also confirmed that cause of death was the single slice across her throat. And, she confirmed the cut as left to right, indicating a right-handed assailant and taller than Penny by several inches."

"Based on our analysis," Rodriguez said, "There were

enough high-velocity spatters to indicate the drop of blood fell from a height consistent with victim and assailant both standing."

"If she would have been kneeling," Hank cut in, "Then we can assume she was forced to do so, which should've been accompanied by defensive wounds. There were absolutely none of those."

"What about the brand on her shoulder?" Karl asked.

"That's something we've made no progress on," Coil said. "Our state crime lab has no references to that type of marking being used in like crimes. They've sent off high-resolution images to the FBI lab and their Behavioral Sciences Unit for profile comparisons. Hank also has close ties to the Bureau and expects to hear back soon." Coil turned so he could address everyone in the room. "I've said it before, but I'll say it again. The information about the branding is highly classified. We do not want that getting out to the public or the press. Am I clear?"

There was a resounding, "Yes, sir," in response.

Coil paced back and forth in the confined space. Hank recognized the pressure and the pain he was under. This was a very close community, murder rarely ever happened.

"It also looks like the killer took off with Penny's keys. They were nowhere onsite, and the front and back door required a key to lock them. Both were locked."

"Was her car stolen?" Karl asked.

"No, it's still in the parking lot out back. We secured a search warrant to look in it, and found nothing but cluttered papers and bills," Coil said.

"How about her trailer?" Deputy Joe Springer asked.

Hank thought Springer's comment odd considering Springer was at Penny's trailer when the search warrant was executed.

Deputy Joe Springer was Bell County's version of

the journeyman cop. He'd bounced from agency to agency with some sort of scandal or dark cloud of allegation following behind him. Nothing ever serious enough for him to be fired or arrested, but just tainted enough to wear out his welcome and intuitive enough to know when to say *adios* before he was asked to leave.

Known as Irish Springer by his friends, Joe looked every bit his native ancestry. A tight shock of red curls framed his pale, freckled face. His eyes were a fierce green that could be guileless enough to make you trust him instantly.

Joe was a wild card, but when he put his mind to it, he was an experienced and solid cop. Of course, the trick was getting him to always put his mind to it.

"What do you mean?" Coil asked him.

"Did you find anything there, or was anything missing?" Springer asked.

"I don't know. It's hard to tell without knowing what was in there to begin with."

"I've heard she hooked up with some guy online," Springer said. "Some war hero coming back from Afghanistan. Last time I saw her at the diner she said he'd be moving in with her. Seems it might be worth checking her computer. Maybe he's our guy."

Hank bit his tongue, but he and Coil exchanged a quick glance. At least they were on the same page.

"We did find a computer," Rodriguez said.

"I'm surprised," Springer said. He went to the coffee pot and filled a Styrofoam cup to the brim.

Hank watched Springer's motions and replayed his questions back in his mind. There was more going on inside that brain than police work. Hank leaned back in his chair and crossed one boot over the other.

"When's the last time you slept with Penny?" Hank asked Springer.

Springer's coffee splashed on his hand and he swore. "Screw you, old man."

"I beg your pardon?" Hank asked, narrowing his eyes.

"I don't know who you are or why you're here, but you're not going to disrespect me like that."

Hank figured the best thing to do was let Coil deal with his men, so he just sat back and watched. Coil took the dry erase marker and flung it across the room so it hit Springer in the back of the head.

"Zip it, deputy, or your next assignment will be scraping cow patties off the road. Since you're not a complete idiot, just process of elimination should tell you if he's in this room, then he's a cop. Or we can all wait while you do a Google search for Hank Davidson and see how many serial killers he's tracked."

"Whatever," Springer said, scowling at Hank. "I don't need this stupid job anyway." He began to remove his badge from his uniform shirt.

"Fine with me," Coil said. "But if you think you're going anywhere without answering his question you can think again. If you think one person in here will protest to see you spend a night behind bars then I think you'll be surprised. Now sit down and answer the question, or I promise your life will be hell."

Springer's face flushed beet red and Hank wondered if the kid was going to go for Coil's throat. He'd never seen a cop with that much built up resentment and anger. He didn't know how he'd passed the psych evaluations.

"I don't even know what he asked," Springer said, smirking.

Hank stood and walked slowly until he was directly in front of Springer, forcing Springer to look up at him.

"When was the last time you slept with Penny? And let me be more specific. When was the last time you slept with her at her house?"

"You mean that rat's nest?" Springer asked, scoffing.

"You obviously didn't mind at the time. So I'll ask one last time."

"Or what?" Springer challenged Hank.

"Or I'll have you cuffed and booked as a suspect in Penny's murder," Coil said. "Please, just try me."

Springer looked like he was finally starting to get the picture that there was no one there to back him up.

"Look," he said, shrugging. "It was nothing. She cut it off when she hooked up with the new guy. No big deal."

"Were you jealous? Maybe a little angry?" Hank pressed.

The look in Springer's eyes was hard. "I ain't jealous of nobody. I served my time overseas. I was regular Army, but combat. I wasn't no SF, but the stuff that guy was telling her didn't make sense. I do know enough about special forces to know he wasn't part of them. I doubt he was even in the Middle East."

"What was his name?" Hank asked

"You think I asked? She said I was out, so I bailed. I'm trying to fix my marriage. I don't have time for that trailer trash."

"You disrespectful, jerk," shouted Karl.

He pushed past Rodriguez and around a table as he steamed toward Springer. Hank saw the emotions of a young man who cared about victims, and who was still reeling from the exposure to death earlier in the day.

"As good as it would feel, it's not worth it, son," Hank said calmly as he stepped in Karl's path.

"Springer," Coil called out.

"What?"

"You still haven't answered the question."

"A week ago."

"Now that wasn't too hard, was it?" Coil asked.

"It's no one's business," Springer said.

"An innocent woman is dead. Don't you think it's our business if you've been sleeping with her and know something about a mystery man? Are you that dense or just that ashamed for running around on your wife?" Coil admonished him.

"I guess you'll be taking my statement as a civilian, because I quit."

Coil just laughed. True genuine laughter in the face of all that anger. "Hold on there, Joe. I know quitting has been your MO since you joined up with Houston PD. Unlike the others you've worked for, I think you have a smidge of talent for this job. But you have a hot head and get fleet feet when a flame is turned up under you. I'm not going to allow you to quit. I'm going to expect you to stand up for that oath you took and stop acting like a baby. You're embarrassing everyone in here who's ever pinned on the badge. Suck it up and do the job."

"What?" Springer asked.

"What?" Karl said at the same time.

Hank could understand where they were coming from. Maybe Coil was just sleep deprived. That kid was nothing but trouble.

Several emotions flitted across Springer's face. Embarrassment and pride, but also gratitude. Had no one ever believed in the kid before? He'd served his country. But what had he come home to?

Without saying a word, Springer took his badge and pinned it back on.

"What makes you think the guy wasn't in the military?" Hank asked him.

"Everything he told her about rank structure, training, and locations was wrong. It sounded more like police rank, but not military structure. And the training he claimed to have is stuff you get off the internet. The things he was saying were a mix SEAL, Ranger, and Raider training. It just doesn't happen like that. Everyone is very specialized in the way they do things."

"That's a great place to start," Hank said.

Chapter Five

TUESDAY

April showers might have brought May flowers, but in Rusty Gun, the rain was rare and the flowers had to rely on a water hose. But they'd had a stretch of rainy days, which she was always grateful for because those were great writing days.

Agatha reluctantly spent an hour on the treadmill in her sunroom. Even throughout the winter, she barely defaulted to the indoor trainer. She was an outdoor runner, no matter the weather. But today was different.

It wasn't as much the weather as it was a general feeling of gloom. She'd run in the rain before. Two days had passed since Hank walked out. She knew she'd hurt him, but apologies weren't on her to-do list. Besides, she'd only told him what was on her heart. If they were going to have a relationship, she should be able to tell him what she's feeling. Otherwise, what was the point.

Coil had reached out the night before about Penny's murder. She felt guilty because it wasn't a secret that Penny wasn't her favorite person, but never in a million years would she wish something so horrible on anyone. She was also hurt, and maybe a little angry, that Hank hadn't bothered to give her a heads up.

It was only eight-fifteen and though she told Coil she'd meet him at his office by ten, there was no way she could sit on her thumbs all morning. Besides, she understood how precious time was. She'd been officially commissioned as a technical consultant on the case. Volunteered of course. Seems Penny's laptop was giving the boys a tough time, and before Coil sent it off to the crime lab's computer forensics unit, he wanted to have her take a crack at it.

Agatha went for the casual look just in case Hank was there. She didn't want him to get the wrong idea that she was trying to dress up for him. Hank didn't go for that anyway. He always appreciated her for who she was.

She wore a pair of khaki cargo pants and a long-sleeve, collared t-shirt in olive green. She laced up her water-resistant boots, and then put on her yellow rain coat to help break up the drab colors.

Agatha steeled her nerves and snatched her keys off the table. Hank or no Hank, she was going in to do a job. She jerked her front door open and crinkled up her nose at the booming thunder and vicious cracks of lightening. Quickly, she peeked across the street to Hank's house, but wasn't able to tell if his BMW was parked in the garage.

"it's just water," she said. "Let's do this."

She hopped down her three concrete steps, and cut a quick left toward her driveway. She didn't have the luxury of a garage like Hank did. Well, actually, she did have a garage, but it was stuffed with her parent's stuff. Since their deaths, she hadn't been able to dispose of or donate anything that reminded her of them. Which was pretty much everything. She'd managed over the years to make the house her own, putting their furniture in storage when the garage could hold no more, and she'd had the floors redone and the rooms repainted. It wasn't the same house she'd grown up in. But the memories were still there.

She hit the unlock button on her key fob and opened the door to her Jeep, hiking herself into the seat while dripping wet.

Something didn't feel right in the car. There was a whistling sound and there was too much noise.

"What the heck?"

Agatha threw off her seatbelt and got up on her knees to look in the back seat. The rear panel of the passenger side rambler seat was torn wide open. The rain had poured into the interior all night and there was standing water along the floorboards. She could pull the plugs to drain the water, but the matts, and the boxes of books she'd planned to donate to the local book store were ruined.

She looked for a downed tree or some debris in the storm that had penetrated the rugged, see-through plastic. But there was nothing visible. There was no use trying to tape it up with a plastic bag while it was raining, and the car couldn't get any wetter, so she started it up and backed out of her driveway. Thank goodness she was driving a Jeep and not something like Hank's BMW.

She drove to the sheriff's office as fast as she could, but high water on the roads and the downpour made everything move slowly. It just didn't make sense about the Jeep being torn up that way. The only way it could have happened was if someone did it on purpose. Maybe some kids messing around.

Coil had texted her to park around back beneath the patio. She smiled for two reasons as she eased next to his Coil's truck. She was grateful the Jeep would be protected, and she noticed Hank's Beemer parked in the front with water halfway up the wheels. Sure, it was petty, but it had been two days without a text or call. He deserved to get a little wet.

She buzzed the back door, and Coil opened it up for her.

"Hey, Agatha. Thanks for coming in so early." Coil handed her a cup of hot tea just how she liked it, and she thanked him.

"I've been up hours," she said, warming her hands on the hot mug. "I just couldn't sit around the house knowing there was work to be done."

"I appreciate it. We've all been at it through the night, but this laptop is beyond us."

Agatha casually looked around the sheriff's office. It wasn't a big space, and she knew Hank was around somewhere. She sensed him. She thought about asking Coil where he'd gone, but she didn't want to seem worried just in case Hank had told them there was tension.

"I got you set up in my office. It's about the only place halfway clean and quiet," Coil said, opening the door.

"You still got that gold in here?" she asked, laughing.

"Unfortunately," he said.

"No way. What's the hold up?"

"Seems everybody is fighting over it. Meanwhile, it remains in my custody. Lucky me."

"Aren't you worried?"

Agatha settled herself behind his desk. She slid the laptop over and powered it up.

"Have you seen that vault? Only three of us know where it is. Hank's too dang big to get in there, and I suppose you'd prefer to avoid the spiders."

"Spiders?" she asked.

Coil's green eyes gleaned in taunting delight as he held his index fingers about four inches apart.

"Big ones

"Do they come out…" she swallowed hard. "Can they get out?"

He smiled. "No, I'm just kidding. Don't need to get you distracted. I really think our killer is inside this stubborn thing. Penny met a guy online. Told her he was military, but his stories didn't add up. We want to look at him hard. I wanted you to peek before I sent it off to Austin."

Coil sipped on his bottle of water.

"You're drinking water?" she asked. "I've never seen you drink water."

"I'm burnt out on coffee. I need the cleanse." There were dark circles under his eyes, and she could tell he hadn't slept.

"What am I looking for?" she asked.

The screen lit up and asked for a password.

"She taped it in the corner," Coil said. "Sometimes being not too bright is a good thing."

"I gotta know," Agatha said, looking up. "Was it bad? I've been hearing rumors about her head severed from the body and all sorts of wild things. I need to know what I'm walking into. I might not have liked her personally, but I've still known her all her life."

"One slice across her throat. Very clean. Very disturbingly professional."

"Ever seen anything like that before?" Agatha asked.

"Never, but I don't have the experience in murder like Hank does, and…"

"It's the cleanest thing I've ever seen," Hank said from the doorway.

Agatha's head jerked to look at him, and she found herself tongue-tied. It was good to see him. They'd rarely gone a day apart since Christmas. He was wearing jeans and a rumpled shirt, and there were circles under the circles beneath his eyes.

"Hank," she said, finally acknowledging him.

"Hello, Agatha." And then he came into the room and sat on the corner of the desk.

She narrowed her eyes. Two could play this game. If he was going to act like there was nothing between them, then she could do the same.

Coil's eyes widened and he took a step back. "Well, I'm going to get out of this room as fast as I can. Call me if you need me."

Coil closed the door behind him.

"So he called you in, huh?" Hank asked. "This is big. Make sure you know what you're getting yourself into."

"What's that supposed to mean?"

"I mean this is an active case, and once you log into that computer, you have become a link in the chain of custody. When an arrest is made, your name becomes part of the trial. This isn't just snooping around old crime scenes, and whoever killed Penny isn't some amateur."

Agatha laid her hand over the lid of the laptop and slowly pressed it closed.

"Smart move," Hank said, smirking a little.

Agatha stood up and walked past him, brushing his knee with her hip. She smiled when she heard him suck in a breath.

"I'm just going to refill my tea."

Chapter Six

Coil called the team together just before lunch. He'd ordered food trays from the local grocery, and knew a working lunch was necessary to keep the momentum going.

Agatha felt a little guilty because she'd actually gotten a few hours of sleep before being called into the case. The others hadn't seen sleep since Monday afternoon.

She sat in a far corner and watched the frenzy, nibbling on her sandwich. She still felt out of sorts and unsure why Coil had requested her in the first place. She wasn't a computer tech geek, and it sure wasn't one of her typical cold cases where she had the time to meticulously examine evidence at her own pace. This was a very fluid and immediate need to catch a killer—a very skilled and dangerous killer.

But the white elephant in the room was Hank Davidson. Forty-eight hours earlier they'd been embraced in each other's arms. Forty-six hours ago, they'd had an emotional exchange that now forced them to sit across the room and pretend to ignore each other.

She knew the importance of not interfering with Hank while he was in the zone. The investigation had about another twenty-four hours before the case began to run cold and clues, witnesses, and leads collapsed. This would be no time for personal issues to arise. This was about finding Penny's killer.

Agatha tossed the remainder of her sandwich and hurried back to Coil's office, but her mind was on Hank. It still made no sense what had happened, but that was the reality of two strong willed people colliding over personal beliefs.

"You find anything?" Coil asked as he stuck his head in.

"I'm in her social media accounts. She's bragging about her man to friends, but other than shadowed images in uniform, there are no clear images of the mystery man."

"Springer doubts his military service, but thinks he could be a cop. Let me know if there's anything we can show him for confirmation either way."

"Will do." Agatha popped open a master search function and stared at the screen.

"How long did you say that she and this guy had been chatting?" she asked.

"Not sure, but I assumed a few weeks." Coil moved into the room and closed the door. "Why?"

Agatha felt a shortness of breath as she scrolled through the messages. She didn't even realize she was touching the left side of her chest, and her fingers rubbed the raised scar.

"Talk to me, Agatha," Coil said. "You don't look so well."

"They've been chatting about a year," she said. "She's spread the dirt on everyone in this town to this guy." Her breath was coming in shorted pants and she knew she had to get control of herself.

"Like what?" he asked. "Small town gossip?"

"No, like all of my personal business."

"Not following."

She felt sick. Penny had betrayed everyone. But mostly her. Why her?

"Penny was being duped." Agatha's voice was hoarse. "All this guy cared about was information and she fed it right to him. Whoever her mystery man is, he has more of a fascination with Rusty Gun than he did with Penny. He never asks about her. When she tries to tell him things he cuts her off. I don't know if he's planning to do something, or just getting a very detailed idea of the town before moving here."

"Is that so bad? Look at Hank. He just up and moved without a place to stay or an idea what a one-horse town this was."

"This is different. I'm seeing a pattern in his lines of questioning."

"Should I get Hank involved?"

"No," she said, louder than she should have.

"Okay, okay." Coil raised his hands in submission.

"This guy asks Penny meaningless stuff about the people and the area, and then asks a specific question about me. Every time."

"He's camouflaging."

"Yes, but she doesn't realize it. He even instructs her to do things. Look," She pointed to the screen, "About a year ago, he told her to ask for my autograph and send the book to him."

"Maybe a big fan?" Coil asked.

"No, this guy is way out of bounds."

"What are the most recent messages? Is he focusing on

you right before he kills her? Maybe she caught on and got jealous or threatened to stop sharing information," Coil suggested.

"He killed her?" Agatha caught onto what he'd said.

"If."

"I think I'm going to be sick." She pressed her hand over her mouth and closed her eyes.

"Enough of you and Hank's spat interfering in this case. I'm calling him in on this," Coil said sternly as he stood to open the office door.

"But, he was the one wh…" she said, trying to defend herself.

Hank jogged over, his face twisted in a concerned scowl.

"What's going on?"

Agatha felt a sense of security with his presence. The intensity of his question assured her that neither fatigue or personal disagreement would deter him from protecting her.

"Agatha has run across something we all need to be aware of. Seems Penny's mystery man was no more than a stalker using her for information about Rusty Gun. But mostly about Agatha."

"His questions grow more specific about me over the last three weeks. He's even directing her to ask about buying or renting my house."

Hank slipped across the threshold and pushed the door shut behind him.

"How'd he know about that?" he snarled.

Agatha pressed against her temple to combat the drum in her head. The more she read, the more reality over-whelmed her. She'd suffered through college because of a stalker who'd almost killed her. She'd left TCU and moved back home because the Fort Worth Police were unable to stop him.

Back then she was a naïve college student who was betrayed by someone she trusted. Her college religion professor felt it was okay to pursue her sexually. When she'd rejected his advances, he decided she'd pay for the rejection.

Agatha tried her best to maintain her grades while looking over her shoulder at every ring of the bell or corner of the campus. Every safety net put in place failed, and it was ultimately up to her to fight for her own life during a late-night attack inside her off-campus apartment.

This was turning out to be the same type of scenario. She'd trusted Penny. Heck, she even spent time with her last Thanksgiving because her grandfather had been murdered by the Santa Serial Killer, Ellie Belle. Yet here she was, again betrayed by an insider. Except she was no longer a naïve college girl.

"Okay, let's see what you got," Hank said. He had a way of speaking with authority that made her feel like he would handle it and everything would be okay.

Agatha kept a firm grip on the laptop.

"Seriously?" Hank asked.

"Agatha," Coil said. "Please don't take this the wrong way, but this isn't some cold case, or a book report. Penny's laptop has got to leave here in a few hours on its way to the geek lab and I've got a very skilled killer to catch. I love you and Hank both as friends, but whatever is going on between y'all is none of my business. And as Sheriff, I cannot allow it to interfere in this investigation."

Agatha knew he was right. But that didn't stop her from becoming even more angry. It had suddenly become too much. She'd never resolved her fear from what happened in that apartment years ago. And although she'd fought for her life and won it back that night, a huge part of her was left on that apartment floor.

"Here," she shoved the laptop across the desk. "I've gotta get my rear window fixed anyway."

"Somebody busted your window?" Coil asked.

Hank ignored her comment while he buried his face in Penny's computer. It aggravated her, but she knew her emotions were running too high. Her past had bubbled just below the surface and it was time to exit before she exploded.

"I think it was the storm," she said.

Coil's cell buzzed and he grabbed it, holding up a finger while his eyes read the screen.

"You okay?" she asked.

Hank's head popped up at the question.

"Seems like more than your Jeep's window is busted. My deputies are heading to your house right now. We got an intruder alert," Coil said, opening the office door.

"But I didn't receive a notice from the monitoring company," she said, but Coil and Hank had already disappeared.

Chapter Seven

"Thanks for waiting outside until we got your house cleared," Coil told her softly.

Hank had waited with her in Coil's truck. The rain was still coming down in sheets, and it didn't look to be stopping anytime soon.

"What's it look like?" Hank asked.

Coil wiped his face with his sleeve. The mixture of rain and sweat from the quick search of her house and property still had him panting for breath.

"It's the darnedest thing. Someone was definitely in your home. I don't know if anything is missing, so you'll have to tell us that or not. But there isn't a trace. That window is smashed in around back, but looks like it was done on purpose."

"On purpose?" Hank asked.

"With all this rain and muck, there's not a drop of moisture or mud anywhere in there except ours. And we came in on the driveway and sidewalk."

"Ghost," Hank whispered. They were all snug inside

Coil's Dodge Ram, and despite the heat being on, Agatha couldn't stop shivering.

"What the heck is going on here?" Agatha asked, her voice sharp.

"This isn't some random fan gone over the edge. If Penny's killer is special forces, we've got a highly skilled assassin on our hands," Hank explained.

"This is all you, Hank. We'll take your lead." Coil turned on the defrost to clear the steamy windows.

Agatha raised her brows at Coil.

"Whoa, what do you mean it's all him? Can't you protect me?"

"Agatha, I come from an undercover world of drug lords and street dealers. This is another realm that Hank has dealt with. It's rare, but I know he's profiled it."

"What do you mean Ghost?" she asked.

"Ghosts are rare, but they commit their lives to killing without a need for recognition. They will not get caught because they are perfect at what they do and how they do it."

"Then how do you know they exist?" she asked.

"In my entire career, I've captured one."

"One?" she asked. "Just one?"

"I'm sorry," he said, shrugging. "I thought you'd want the truth."

"So I'm a dead woman?"

"Never. We'll protect you day and night," Coil said.

"For how long? This ghost has been planning this for over a year. He knows everything about me thanks to that moron, Penny. She got what she deserved." Agatha punched the dashboard.

Hank put his arm around her shoulder. "Now, come on, Aggie. Penny wasn't maliciously setting you up. She paid for her mistake with her life."

Agatha curled forward in sobs. "I can't do this again. I can't…I can't. I can't go back home."

"Let me call Nick Dewey. I'm sure we can use that place in Fort Worth he lent to us during the Ellie Belle case last Christmas."

"We'll keep you safe," Coil said. "If this guy is in Rusty Gun, he can't hide forever without someone stumbling over him. Everyone is too nosy."

"The question is," Hank asked. "Why you?"

She wiped her eyes and tried to find what was left of her strength deep inside her. "I've no idea," she said.

"No, seriously, what have you done to capture some-one's attention? I'm not insinuating anything, but ghosts don't pick at random. They may track their target over a lifetime. It's not the number of kills that counts. It's the motivation for killing. See, ghosts don't start out as killers. They get the idea, which then becomes the obsession. Instead of acting on the impulse, they explore every possi-bility of getting caught. So they plan and practice until they've mastered a script."

"I really have no idea," she said. "Maybe he's got PTSD and hated one of my books."

"He's not military. Springer looked through the text files again and he's certain the guy doesn't know jack about military rank structure or training, much less special forces," Coil said.

"So who is he?" she demanded.

"Springer said he's a cop. Maybe. He thought he was telling Penny military details, but it's actually law enforce-ment stuff such as rank structure, chain-of-command, and training."

"But I'm friends with every cop I meet," she said. "I've worked with dozens of cops all over the country."

"Maybe you were too friendly and they felt jilted," Hank suggested.

"Jilted?" she whispered. Her fingers touched the scar over her left breast again.

"Maybe, he's not a cop. Maybe he's just institutionalized. Prisoners become very familiar with law enforcement. They've nothing better to do, so they watch. And they learn," Hank said.

She could feel Hank watching her closely, seeing how she reacted to the things he was saying. But she was numb inside. She couldn't fathom the possibilities.

"Good point," Coil said. "Plus, I can't see a cop being so careful about a crime scene, yet leaving a mark on his target. Doesn't add up."

"Using a brand is an evolved need," Hank said. "Ghosts are slow, methodical, and highly intelligent. Not just intelligent, but educated as well."

"What's the difference?" Coil asked.

"It doesn't require an education to be intelligent, but it does take intelligence to be educated. They need the accolades of degrees and diplomas to satiate their fragile, yet super-inflated ego."

Agatha's heart began to pound and she went clammy. Sweat broke out on her brow and black spots dances in front of her eyes. She had to get out of the truck. She needed air.

She fumbled for the car door handle and fell out into the rain, letting the cold drops sizzle off her skin. She didn't care that she was laying in her driveway. She just closed her eyes and let the rain come down.

Hank knelt beside her and she wanted to smile as he felt her pulse.

"Agatha, you're ice cold," he said. "Do we need to call an ambulance?"

She shook her head. "You said brands."

"Yeah," Coil said, kneeling on her other side. "Like Penny."

"I never saw the pictures from the crime scene. She was branded?" She could hear the edge of hysteria in her voice.

Hank lifted her up and held her loosely in his arms, protecting her from some of the rain with his body. They were all wet. What did it matter?

She tried to sit up, but she was weak as a newborn calf. But she knew what had to be done. Her fingers trembled as she tried to unzip her raincoat. Hank helped her pull it off. Neither of them asked anymore questions. They just placated the whims of a woman who was losing her mind.

The buttons of her shirt were too hard to work, and frustration got the better of her, so she tore the shirt over her head, so she sat before them in her sports bra. She moved the strap to the side.

"Did it look like this?" she asked.

It was a raised scar from a burn in the shape of a cruci-fix. She'd once been branded.

Hank's grip on her tightened and she could feel his tremors of rage.

Coil just stared and finally said, "Yes."

"I know who he is," she said.

Chapter Eight

THE SHERIFF'S Office was packed. Detectives, Texas Rangers, a probation officer, and federal agents were mostly courteous about making space for each other. Greetings were sparse, but a general recognition was obvious. It was a serious and somber setting with no place for chit-chatting.

Agatha was back in her familiar corner of the room, but she felt no comfort from the familiarity. She watched Hank move amongst his tribe. She was happy for him, but also saddened because she knew once this was resolved, the crew of detectives would return to their desk with loads of open cases, and he'd go back to watering his roses.

Coil tapped her on the shoulder. She jerked and looked up, but at least she tried to offer him a smile, strained as it was. He handed her a bottle of water.

"This is going to get raw," he said. "If you need my office at any time, it's open for you."

Agatha nodded and patted him on the hand. He was worried about her. He should be.

Lieutenant Maria Rodriquez was assigned to her, and

she was under strict orders to never leave her side. Rodriguez smiled at Agatha, but in reality, there was no way anyone could know what she was going through without having experienced it too.

"Can I have a moment?" Hank asked Rodriguez.

"Sure, Detective," she said and gave him her seat.

Hank sighed and took Agatha's hand just like he had before their fight. "I'm so sorry about all of this."

"It's okay. We're just two strong-willed people with differing opinions. There's no reason not to be civil with each other. We're still friends, right?"

Hank looked down and appeared to have trouble collecting his thoughts. Agatha gave him time to reflect because she knew how hard it probably was for him. Hank had a lot of pride, and apologies probably didn't come easy.

"Umm," he said, "I'm talking about this case."

"Oh."

Embarrassed, she guzzled from her water bottle.

"I knew you'd been stalked and forced into a reclusive lifestyle, but I had no idea you almost died, or that you'd been marked. I wouldn't have asked because I respected your privacy."

Agatha considered his words and realized that as close as they'd grown, she had never actually told him, or anyone for that matter. Coil knew some of it because he'd accessed her case file, but he'd assured her it was no one else's business and he'd only looked at the surface. But she felt a little angry.

"You know, Hank, remember before Christmas when you got mad because everyone respected your privacy about Tammy's murder. No one ever bothered to ask. They never asked if you needed to talk about it, or what you were feeling. They just let you carry all that pain on your own, and it hurt you."

"It did," he agreed.

"Then you have no excuse," she said, her voice sharp. "Stop being so stinking respectful of my privacy and ask me what happened that night."

Hank didn't look surprised at her outburst, but he did squeeze her hand a little tighter. They were surrounded by people.

He leaned closer. "What happened that night?"

Agatha exhaled, the tears welling behind her eyes. How long she'd wanted someone to ask her that question.

"Thank you," she said softly, letting the tears fall. "Ask me again when we're alone. I don't think I can do this in a crowd of people. I'm not sure what it'll do to me."

Hank nodded and pulled her into his arms for a hug. "That's a deal. I've got to get back to work. Rodriguez will take good care of you."

Coil signaled that the briefing was about to start. A knot in her gut had her shifting in her seat. Maybe it wasn't a good idea to sit in on the briefing. It was her life that was about to be on exhibit for all to see. She hadn't felt that helpless since the night in her apartment when Salt had attacked her.

"You okay?" Rodriguez asked.

"I've had better days."

"I bet. If I were you I'd already be through a couple bottles of wine by now."

Agatha managed a smile.

"I want to thank everyone for coming in on such short notice," Coil said. "I've given everyone a briefing sheet with all of the details as we know them. We feel like we've got a solid identity on our killer. We'll find it's the same person who broke into Agatha Harley's home earlier today.

You'll see in your pages that Ms. Harley was an initial victim of Dr. Ray Salt over eighteen years ago while he was a professor and she was a student at TCU."

Her stomach twisted at the sound of Salt's name. She hadn't spoken it in all those years. She'd also never forgotten it.

Agatha couldn't leave the briefing for the safety of Coil's office, as much as she wanted to. She'd left college for the safety of her parents' home, but that had only left her alone. She wasn't hiding anymore.

Coil popped Salt's latest prison mug shot up on the projector screen. "What we also know is that Salt should still be in prison. What we don't know is why he's out."

A wiry man about mid-forties with a slick bald head and a goatee that looked like it was an effort to compensate for no skull coverage raised his hand. Agatha disliked him immediately.

"I'm Parole Officer Daniel Appleton. I was told to be here by my supervisor, so I'll try to help you with that." He adjusted a thick-rimmed pair of black eyeglasses.

"Is Salt in your case load?" Coil asked.

"Yeah," Appleton said, "Why else would I be here?"

"Well, you said you were told to be here. So that doesn't naturally mean you wanted to be here, seeing Salt is your responsibility," Coil replied coolly.

Appleton shoved his hand in the pocket of a crumpled pair of khaki cargo pants. He jerked out an E-cigarette from his pocket. He began to load some type of liquid vaping product into it.

"Not in here, Appleton," Coil said.

Appleton flipped his wrist at Coil's words.

"Look, I know how this junk goes. You're all wanting to blame this on somebody from the state. I'm not going to be your whipping boy. I got enough cases to deal with. Salt is a good guy. He just got caught up," Appleton claimed.

"Care to explain?" Coil asked, his voice frigid.

"The guy applied for post-conviction relief. His attorney was able to twist it off over a technicality. The guy got cut loose with credit for good time served. Salt set up a program while inside to help cons get their GEDs, so the state shined a good light on him."

"When did he walk?" Coil asked.

"Over a year ago."

Agatha watched the exchange as if it were an out-of-body experience. How in the world could anyone say the words Salt and good man in the same sentence?

"Why wasn't the victim notified of the offender's release?" Coil asked.

Appleton's face flushed red, and he shrugged. "The chick moved away. Heard she ran off to hide because she was too embarrassed. She didn't update her victim notification information, so what am I supposed to do, track her down to tell her that her ex-boyfriend, the professor was free?"

"Are you for real?" Coil asked. "You can't be that much of a scumbag."

Appleton stood as if to challenge Coil.

"Hey, man. If you don't want my help just say so. This hole in the wall town ain't where I want to spend my evening."

The tension in the room ramped up so fast that Agatha thought paint would peel.

"Do you understand that your friend, the professor almost killed a college girl?" Coil asked. "If it hadn't been for the blender she smashed against his skull, he would've killed her."

"How do you know?" Appleton asked. "Just because she said it don't make it true."

"Because he branded her with the same mark that he branded Monday's victim with. That's his MO before killing."

"Hey, what do you expect? The college chick was consensual until she decided it was easier to blame Ray than it was to explain why she flunked out of our class to her folks." Appleton stuck the electronic cigarette in his mouth. It hung from between his lips with the help of his index finger. "I've seen it a million times. This chick wasn't no different."

Agatha's eyes filled with tears.

"Don't do it, hun," Rodriguez said. "Don't give him the satisfaction. Dry your eyes."

Before she knew what was happening Hank was front and center, and his fist slammed into Appleton's jaw, sending the E-cigarette across the room and Appleton to the floor.

"Well, ladies and gentlemen," Coil said. "It looks like Parole Officer Appleton ran right into the wall. Clumsy of him."

Chapter Nine

HANK PEEKED through the living room blinds. Again. The four officers assigned to Agatha were still on duty.

Hank rubbed his forehead, the tension of the night catching up with him. He knew that although the officers were committed, those watch duties always went to rookies. He'd have rested easier had there been a SEAL team, but that wasn't even a remote possibility. He was solely responsible for Agatha's safety.

"Would you relax?" Agatha asked. "You're making me nuts."

"I wish I could, but the reality is, it's going to be up to us to protect us. Those rookies mean well, but they've never seen anything like this."

Agatha was curled up on the couch with a glass of wine. It was just before midnight and she'd finally begun to wind down. She still had on yoga pants and an oversized t-shirt, but her shoes were kicked off between the sofa and glass coffee table.

A light brush against a window on the south side of

Hank's home caused a spike of adrenaline to set his mind and body in motion.

"Well, that didn't take long," he said.

"What?"

"That noise. You know the plan. You wait in the panic room until I signal the all clear."

Agatha jumped to her feet, but she was woozy. Between the exhaustion and the wine, he was surprised she was upright.

"I am not about to hide in the closet like a child during a thunderstorm."

Hank heard the sound again and waved her back.

"I'm not hiding in your panic room. You probably don't even have snacks in there."

He rolled his eyes, debating whether or not it was worth the argument. "There's a snub nose revolver in the end table."

"There's a Glock .9mm in my gym bag."

"Good Lord," he said, throwing up his hands. The woman was making him crazy.

Hank moved quickly to the other end of the house, and sliced through the darkened sections of his home by memory. He stuck close to the wall but was careful not to touch it. He knew it would make enough noise for an outside intruder to hear. He waited and allowed his own breathing to calm. There was no more noise outside. Maybe it was the wind or one of the deputies relieving himself.

He heard Agatha gasp. It was slight and subtle, but Hank trusted what he'd heard. Had he been tricked with a diversion so Agatha would be left alone? Fool woman. That's why he'd wanted her in the panic room.

Hank had custom installed the room after he'd purchased the house. He didn't trust a contractor with the knowledge of what he had stored in his home. It was better he do it himself. The room was a reinforced sanctuary. The walls were bullet and fire proof, and he had installed a separate console to control the video surveillance systems throughout the house and around his property. It had taken him months, but it was just as he wanted it.

None of that mattered now because Agatha's mule-headedness had led her into whatever danger she was now in. Hank had half a mind to let her stew in the mess she'd created, but his heart and soul said no way would he ever allow anyone to harm her again.

Hank began to retrace his steps. His Springfield Armory 911, .45 caliber semi-automatic pistol set snug at his right grip, while he held a home controller in his left. He heard light, almost casual talking, but it wasn't surprising that Agatha would remain calm in a life or death scenario. What he was sure of was that she wasn't alone.

Hank's steps quickened but his vision remained focused along the low-profile combat style three-dot tritium site custom mounted on his weapon. The eerie green glow made taking aim at his target much more accurate.

He turned the last corner before the open area living room. It would be a hard space to remain tactically safe, so Hank flipped the hard plastic cover with his left thumb and mashed a master control.

The lights in the entire house went out. The home, with all of the shutters closed was pitch black on the inside. Hank didn't hesitate to continue moving forward toward the threat. He calmly reached above his brow and flipped on the NVG toggle switch.

The fourth-generation Night Vision Goggles allowed Hank a distinctive advantage over anyone in the house.

His image looked like a crystal clear green pea soup color, but he was immediately able to make out faces and actions.

He swallowed twice before he turned the corner into his living room. He wasn't sure what carnage to expect, but he'd learned to not be affected by anything as it was all going down. Quick, silent, and deadly was his plan. And he was good at his plan.

He spotted Agatha. She appeared unharmed. He moved his head to the right and saw two men. Both held their hands up high. There were no weapons in them. He continued to move across the far end of the room until he was satisfied there were no others.

"Will? Whitehorse?" Hank said. "Is that you?

"Friendlies, here to help," Will Ellis called out.

He turned off the NVG power switch and hit the lights.

"What in the heck are y'all doing? I could've shot you," Hank said.

"Naw, I had their backs," Coil said. He was standing across the room and concealed behind a support beam's post.

Hank holstered his weapon. He was as relieved as he was angry.

"Y'all think this is funny?" Hank asked.

"Whoa," Coil said with his hands lifted in surrender. "We needed to talk with y'all in private and also test your security."

"It stinks," Whitehorse said. Detective-Sergeant Jason Whitehorse had become a friend after they'd started out on shaky terms. Hank now trusted the man, and knew he'd always have his back.

"We slipped right past those rookies and your security, Hank," Will said. His smile said he wasn't even sorry.

"As happy as I am to see you boys, I'm really disappointed my security system didn't pick you up."

"It's cool," Whitehorse said. "We've all operated on federal Red Teams used to test facilities like nuclear plants and military installations. We always go undetected."

"Good news for you, but not really for us. What is it that you had to come here to say?"

Hank was still unhappy with what had happened, but he did recognize that his friends had special skill sets. While his were investigations and criminal profiling, their specialties were covert operations. Will though, was just along for the ride.

"We think there's a fox in the hen house," Whitehorse said.

"Appleton?" Hank asked.

Whitehorse nodded.

"How?"

Whitehorse pointed to Will. Will coughed to clear his throat. He, like all of them, looked physically exhausted.

"While Appleton and Coil were arguing, I noticed he said that Agatha had failed our course. He's not much older than Agatha, so I thought maybe they'd been in school together. I checked enrollment and sure enough, Daniel Appleton was not only a student of Salt's, but he was working toward his master's degree with Salt as his thesis advisor while Appleton served as his graduate assistant."

"I'm not surprised," Agatha said. "But I don't recall him."

"I'm sure you two ran in different crowds," Hank said.

"Once Salt was arrested, Appleton dropped out of school and went to work as a state Parole Officer."

"What's the draw to Salt? Were they lovers?" Hank asked.

"Why would Salt have pursued me if he wasn't into women?" she asked.

"Too simple," Hank said. "You're avoiding the reality. He didn't desire you as a lover, he hated you because you're a woman. The burning cross is either religious symbolism or a re-enactment of the Salem witch burnings," Hank suggested. "But, since I didn't get a chance to interview him or review his records, I'm only guessing."

"So, Appleton is a jealous lover who has helped him exact revenge on the woman who took them away from each other?" Will asked.

"Not sure sexual preference is at play here. I think it's much deeper than that," Hank said. "We'll see how he behaves tomorrow."

"No way," Agatha said. "I don't want him anywhere near us."

"What better way to find Salt," Whitehorse said.

Hank finally holstered his weapon. "Keep your friends close, and your enemies closer."

"Exactly," Will said.

"You better let the rookies know before you walk out of here," Agatha said.

Whitehorse made a sound like a spooky ghost. "They'll never know."

Chapter Ten

"It sure is weird without Penny working here," Agatha said. She looked around the café at the light crowd of folks.

"Yeah," Hank said. "Karl said his mom wasn't sure if she'd reopen the Brisket Basket."

Agatha smiled at the older lady who also filled in at the café back when Penny's grandfather had been murdered. She wasn't the best, or the most accurate, but it appeared she was available to work the day shift.

"Hey, there's Deputy Springer." Agatha waved him over, and the man strutted across the place. She could tell Hank wasn't happy and immediately regretted inviting him.

"Davidson," Springer said.

"Springer," Hank responded.

"I'm your shadow today," Springer said to Agatha. "I just wanted to say hello."

Agatha understood what he meant. In her briefing with Coil, there would be levels of officers assigned to protect her. Some were obvious and in uniform, while others would keep their distance and remain in plain clothes. That also explained why Springer was in an old pair of denim jeans and a tattered flannel unbuttoned over a Captain America t-shirt.

"I appreciate it," Agatha said, giving him a smile.

"Well, anyway, I just wanted to say hello." Springer sipped from his coffee mug and stood there awkwardly. Agatha kicked Hank from under the table.

"Good call on our suspect," Hank said.

"Sir?" Springer asked, confused..

"We were stuck on a suspect with a military connection. You nailed it with the police or institutionalized idea. It was a good call. You've got good instincts."

Springer nodded in appreciation and then faded back to the other side of the café where he could keep watch.

Agatha smiled. "I'm proud of you, Hank. You were the bigger man."

"I only wanted to give credit where credit is due. The guy's got great instincts, he's just trapped in his own skin."

"Aren't we all?" she asked.

"I guess so, but it doesn't mean we can't shed."

"Like a snake?" Agatha shivered at the thought. She hated snakes.

"That's one way to look at it. Point is, we all come wrapped in something that's usually a product of the life we knew. It doesn't prevent us from finding what else is below."

"Wow, that's pretty deep."

"It's the truth. We can grow. Now it doesn't mean we will or that we even want to, but it's there if you want it badly enough."

Agatha suddenly felt a shade of shame. She felt like he was holding a mirror up to her and she was mocking not him, but what she should've seen reflected back at her.

"You're talking about me, aren't you?" she asked.

"No, I was talking about people in general. I respect your opinions, and although I may not agree with them, they indeed are yours to carry the blessings or the burdens of those same opinions."

"Have you been reading some self-help book, because this doesn't sound like you at all."

"Not lately, but I'm not some meathead cop, Aggie. It's what you think of me, I get it, but it doesn't mean that's what I am."

His eyes held intensity framed by a sadness in his face. She knew she'd hurt him, but she didn't know what to do to make it better.

"I do not," she protested.

"You all but said it—I'm a trigger puller. It's disappointing you only see that, but it doesn't make it true. It's only true for you."

Agatha shifted uncomfortably in her usually cozy, padded booth seat. "I'm not sure what's going on here, but while I appreciate the new Gandhi, I don't know why you think I've got a problem with you."

"You implied I was a killer," Hank said. The anger in his voice was unmistakable.

"I never called you a killer. I know you do what you have to for the job."

"You said I enjoyed it."

"That was my impression." They were locked in an inescapable conflict with the very same man she felt most close to. "Did you?"

"I enjoy living," Hank said. "If that means killing someone who's trying to kill me, then heck yeah I'm going to kill them. I'd think you'd understand that better than anyone."

"It's still about killing."

"It's about being free." He exclaimed.

"I'll come back later," the waitress said, her eyes big as she backed away.

"They're here," Hank said. Coil, Will and Whitehorse had just come in.

"Good," she snarled.

"Just in case you're wondering, my duty to protect the public overrides anything I might be feeling at this moment," Hank said.

"What's that supposed to me..." Agatha was cut off by arrival of the others.

"Good to see everyone a little more rested," Coil said. "The folks here are wearing me out demanding answers. I don't blame 'em, but I think it's best we keep it quiet until we know for sure."

"What do you mean, know for sure?" Agatha challenged him.

She felt her blood boiling. It was one of those days where every conversation would end in an argument. It wasn't that she was looking for fights, but somehow deep inside, she couldn't help it.

"We have to look at the facts as we know them. There is still a criminal case to prove. I know we know it's Salt, but there is no evidence linking him to Penny's murder," Coil explained.

"Or the break-in at your house," Will added.

She threw her hands up and exhaled, "So he gets away again?"

"What are you referring to, gets away again? When did he get away the last time?" Coil asked.

"He walked away from prison," she said. "Now I'm a prisoner in my own town."

"We were talking," Coil said. "And we think it's be best for you to leave town until we can piece this together."

"No," she said.

"Ma'am, this isn't the time for personal redemption," Whitehorse said. "Penny deserves a justice that you were given as a gift—life."

"So you're saying I'm making this all about me, and that I don't care about Penny?" she asked.

"I don't seem to be as afraid of hurting you by telling the truth as these guys do," Whitehorse said. "I guess it's because I don't know you, but all we've done of late is make sure you're okay." Whitehorse held up his hands to stop her from exploding. "We've not done one bit of actual investigations work to tie Salt to Penny. Let's say we grab Salt as he walks into this restaurant. Then what? He's done nothing wrong, and thanks to a decision made by a liberal parole board, he has paid his debt to society and to you, Agatha. So, he is still free and clear to do and go as he pleases. Unless we actually start doing police work, and hang Penny's murder on him."

"I'll come back later," the waitress said again, hearing the last of the conversation.

Agatha nodded. "You're right. I've been selfish. And while I'd never dream of interfering, I've done just that." Agatha waved at the waitress for her check. "I'll leave for a safe house."

Agatha pushed Will out from his seat so she could get up from the table. She was determined to do whatever was needed to put Salt away. Even if it meant getting out of the way.

"Hang on," Coil said. "I have Lieutenant Rodriguez on her way to escort you."

"No need," she said

"But, Aggie?" Hank reached out.

"It's okay, Hank. I don't want to interfere with your job to protect the public," she said, throwing his words back at him. She pulled her hand away from his and walked toward the door. She could feel the pressure building inside her, like steam in a tea kettle. If she could only escape all the eyes she could breakdown in private. Then no one would know how weak she was.

She saw Springer getting ready to hop up, but she pointed her finger at him and shook her head no. She saw him look behind her to Coil. He sat back down. She shoved the glass door open and heard the metal chimes clang above her head. Agatha stopped on the sidewalk beneath the metal awning. She spotted Karl Johnson in a track suit, but his look of guilt just told her he was also assigned to follow her.

She stepped to the side when she heard the café door open behind her.

"What is going on with you?" Hank asked.

"I told you," she said. "I'm fine. Go away."

"You're not fine. You don't stand a chance out here. Yeah, you beat him once, but things are different now. He's planned this for years, and you've seen how he operates. He's a ghost."

"Then I'm a ghostbuster." Her breaths were heaving in her chest. Maybe she was having a heart attack. Everything inside of her hurt.

"You can't be serious? You're much smarter than this. You're acting like a spoiled child," Hank said. "Do you have a death wish?"

"No," she yelled, finally exploding. She turned around and shoved him a step back. "How can I have a death wish when I died that night."

She didn't realize she was sobbing.

Hank pulled her into his arms and held her.

"How can you say that?" he asked. "You're a survivor. Look at the amazing things you've done with your life."

"Really? And you know all about my life? You know the fear and pain I shove down every day just so I can keep moving forward. You think it's easy going out of my house and pretending that Salt or some other freaking maniac isn't going to be there waiting to finish the job?"

"Aggie," he said, kissing the top of her head. "I'm sorry, I didn't know."

"I told you I didn't trust Penny asking all those questions. My instincts were right. But I was overreacting. No one believed me."

"I believed you," he said.

"I can't keep living this way," she said, pulling out of his grasp. "If he wants me, he can come and get me."

Chapter Eleven

AGATHA PUSHED out of Hank's grasp just in the nick of time. The glass door shattered behind them and a loud crack rent the air. Hank grabbed Agatha with his left hand and drew his weapon with his right. He jerked her off her feet as they dove behind a line of cars parallel parked in front of the café.

Hank felt the weight of her body in flight crash down upon his, and she grunted at the impact. His right shoulder caught the brunt of the fall. It felt like a branding iron had been shoved through his muscle.

"You okay?" he rasped, scrambling to cover her body with his own.

"I think so," she said.

"Get behind this front tire. The engine block will help protect you. Unless you still want to go out there on your own."

He was in agonizing pain. He wasn't sure if it was the dive for cover or a bullet. He wiped his hand across his right shoulder and triceps. There was no blood.

Hank struggled to his knees. He couldn't lift the weight

of the pistol with his right arm. A quick switch from right to left and he was back in the fight. Another round from the rifle slammed into the side of the car they used as cover. The sound came from the same direction as the first attempt. Hank aimed his gun in that direction, but he knew the .45 would never match the distance or accuracy of a high-powered rifle.

Agatha's eyes were huge, like dinner plates, and her skin was still flushed from the sudden lunge behind the vehicle. She had a naturally pleasant expression as a default, but Hank saw the tension of fear etched into the waning smile. She was a warrior poet in every sense of the word.

"Where's Coil?" she asked.

"They're pinned down inside along with Springer. We've got to coordinate with Karl. He's across the street on the shooter's side."

"How do you know where the shooter is?" Agatha asked.

"You can see where the bullet struck the restaurant's floor right there," he said nodding. Look at the direction. That's why we're on this side for cover and not the other."

"Are you serious? In that micro-second under gun fire, you saw and thought about all of that?"

"Yep. We're no good without information, so I grabbed all that I could before we scrambled."

Pain was causing him to grow weak, so he rested on his heels while he fought to catch his breath.

"I guess you really are as good as they say," she said.

"Not good enough. We need help getting out of here."

"How about him?" she asked, pointing.

Hank looked over his shoulder and saw Deputy Springer sprinting from around back of the café and across the street to join Karl. The guy was nuts crossing without cover fire, but Hank knew his motivation. His partner was out there alone.

"I told you the guy had potential," Hank said.

"Yeah, but he's gotta live to experience it."

"I know this isn't the best time to talk about it, but we've got no place to go until we've been given the all-clear. But I wish you trusted me enough to tell me all that happened with Salt. I feel like there's more to it. I understand how terrifying it is to be stalked, but you smashed his brains in with that blender. You're a fighter and you won. Why the constant fear?"

"How much do you really know about Salt's MO?" she asked.

They both ducked at the sound of another shot. This one was from a distance. Hank knew it was a cover shot to keep pursuers at bay. Still, they drew closer together.

"Enough to know he's a threat and needs to be stopped."

"Do you remember when we first worked the Natalie Green case?"

"Sure. It was our first case."

"That was the first time I opened up to you about my situation. You said if he ever came back around, and I wanted you to, that you'd kill him for me."

Hank closed his eyes, trying to battle back the darkness. The pain in his shoulder was unbearable. He sucked in a deep breath through his teeth and then exhaled.

"I remember," he said.

"I want you to."

"Tell me the truth. The whole truth, Aggie."

She curled up into a tight ball with her back against the car and her arms wrapped around her knees. She looked so small and delicate. Fragile.

"He raped me. Not that night, but over that semester. I

66

was a teenage girl from this small town. I didn't know what to do or who to call. I moved off campus thinking an apartment would help me hide. Then he found me and said he was coming to tutor me—again."

Hank felt rage burn deep in the pit of his stomach. There were no words he could say that could comfort her.

"You were right about the branding being religious. He said I was a harlot for having unmarried sex with him. I was asleep when he arrived because I'd been sick all evening. Then I heard the crash. I couldn't take it anymore, Hank, I just couldn't. I went to the kitchen for a knife and that's where he blindsided me. I missed the knife as we both went to the floor, but I did grab the blender.

"He was on top of me, tearing my t-shirt, but this time instead of crying, I just got still. I put everything I had into it and swung that thing as hard as I humanly could. It shattered when it connected with his skull. I can still hear the sound in my head."

Hank gritted his teeth through the extreme pain and lifted his injured right arm to hold her.

"You were pregnant," he said quietly.

"Why would you say that?" she asked, looking up at him.

"You've said before that you never throw up. But you just said you had been sick all evening."

"I never reported the sexual assaults to the police," she said. "But I reported the stalking to the police and the school. He'd been doing the same thing to girls for years, but it was always covered up because of bad publicity and he was a tenured professor. But he kept little souvenirs. They found all kinds of stuff when they raided his apartment. He pled guilty to several counts of stalking and sexual assault, and he pled guilty to aggravated burglary. They told me he'd do at least twenty-five years, but I guess

LILIANA HART & LOUIS SCOTT

they were wrong about that." She laughed but there was no humor in it.

"I never reported the rapes. Even when all the other girls started coming forward. I didn't want him to know about the baby. I was afraid he'd find her."

"You had the baby?" he asked.

"Yes," she smiled sadly. "She was adopted by a family from San Antonio."

"I'm so proud of you for trusting me with this. I'll never betray that trust." Hank eased her closer and kissed the top of her head.

"I'm sorry I'm telling you this now. I guess just in case we don't make it out of here alive, I didn't want to keep anything from you."

"This isn't a deathbed confession. We're getting out of here alive."

Hank rolled from his seated position and collapsed against the car and sidewalk. The pain and adrenaline had become too much. He let the pistol slide across his thigh until it rested between his legs.

Agatha grabbed the gun, "I got us covered, Hank."

"Hank, come in." Coil's voice came across the police radio Hank had stuffed in his pocket.

"This is Agatha," she said

"Y'all okay?"

"I think Hank's shoulder is dislocated, but we're okay. Can you get us out of here? We're sitting ducks. And Hank looks like he's about to pass out."

"Working on it. Karl and Springer are still clearing the opposite side of the street. Will and Whitehorse went out back to lock down a perimeter, and I'm in the café with a boatload of frightened customers."

Hank smiled as he watched her take over. They really

had become good partners. Sharing each other's strengths and weaknesses was what teamwork was about.

"Sheriff, this is Karl." Hank listened to the police radio conversations.

"Go Karl." Coil said.

"Springer and I came to the far end of town, and don't see anything around. But…"

"But what?"

"Weirdly enough, there's a man on a horse."

Chapter Twelve

"I'm okay," Hank said grunting. He tried to sit up from the gurney. It was as wide as a popsicle stick and as cold as if it had just come out of the freezer.

"The doctor said another hour until the meds level off. Then we can go home."

Hank blinked a few times. He thought that was Agatha's voice, but it sounded like she was laughing into a bucket of sand. The more he struggled to sit up, the faster his head spun.

"Home. Now."

"Okay, caveman," a man said. "Just settle down."

He recognized Coil's voice.

The bleeps on the bedside monitor began to jump and beep rapidly. Hank's heart rate raced up the scale and sweat began to pour from his forehead. He felt the shift from woozy to full-on alert. His hands gripped the adjustable rails of the bed and he knew he had to get up. To get out.

"Hank, you've got to stop," Coil said.

"They're poisoning me." Hank's words were slurred.

"No, Hank. You're okay." Agatha stroked his head with a wet towel.

Coil moved closer so Hank could focus on his face. "The old doc delivered all of my and Shelly's babies. He's good as gold. I promise."

"Am I having a baby? I don't want one. We gotta get out of here." Hank's desperate pleas turned into threatening rumbles. "Get these wires out of me." He grabbed at an IV and the chest monitors.

"Hank Davidson, you stop that right now," Agatha said, using her sternest voice.

He relinquished the fight. He'd take another approach, but either way, he was going to escape.

"Sure, mom, I'll be good." He tried to chuckle, but he felt saliva slip across his chin.

"How you feeling, buddy?" Coil asked.

Hank's vision had begun to clear, and he now knew who was saying what. His mind was still in a fog, but even at fifty percent, Hank's deductive reasoning was one hundred percent sharper than most people.

"I'm fine." Hank felt the constricted movement and glanced over to see the sling that had his right arm tucked snuggly against his body.

"Doc Cartwright says your shoulder popped out," Coil said. "And there might be a tear in your rotator cuff. That'll take an MRI, so for now, just keep that arm immobilized."

"Cartwright? Is that Heather's dad?" Hank asked.

"Yeah, you've met him before," Agatha said.

"Does he know?" Hank said, giggling. He'd never heard that sound come out of his mouth before, but he kind of liked it.

"Know about what?" Agatha asked.

"His little darling and Deputy Karl doing the nasty."

LILIANA HART & LOUIS SCOTT

"Hank, you must still be loopy," Coil said. "You should probably zip it."

"It's the truth," Hank persisted. "Karl's mama is sure mad about it. Says Heather's the devil."

"Hey Hank?"

"Yeah Reggie?" he giggled again.

"Shut up."

"Okiedokie. Did I ever tell you what I did to your pillow at the National Academy?" Hank asked, laughing even harder

"No, what did you do?" Coil asked.

"Hank, why don't you just hush and rest now," Agatha said, her lips twitching. "You're about to get in a whole mess of trouble."

"You're right, Aggie. No need spilling the beans." Hank's words continued to slur.

"Wait," Agatha said, caught up in the silliness. "We changed our minds. Tell us everything."

"Horsey," Hank whispered.

"He's fruit loops," Coil said. "Wish I'd been recording it."

"We have to go," Hank said. "I have a horse to catch. And then I have to have this baby. Doc Cartwright's going to deliver it."

"You can catch the horse in the morning," Coil said, chuckling. "I can't help you with the baby."

"Just like a man," Hank said.

"And how's the patient?" A deep, graveled voice asked from farther away.

"He's lost his mind," Agatha said. "I kind of like it."

Hank strained to open his eyes. He needed to wake from this fog. There was work to do. He had to catch the horse thief. Or maybe a killer. He wasn't sure. But he needed to get up and out.

"How you feeling, son?" Doc asked.

"Frisky."

"I'm sure the lady is thrilled to hear it."

The old town doctor looked frail, but at seventy-four years old, he still jogged every morning, practiced yoga and ate healthy. His mind remained sharp, but if there was major surgery to be conducted, he referred his patients to his younger colleagues. The people of Rusty Gun were thankful for that decision.

Hank reached for Agatha. "Are you thrilled to hear it?" he asked, waggling his eyebrows.

She laughed and said, "Do you think you can sedate him?"

"Sure thing," Doc laughed.

"You're going to go home in an hour, but I'll schedule an MRI for that rotator. It's nothing to play with. The bruising along your rib cage looks like a piano fell on top of you."

Coil burst out laughing.

"Sedate him too" Agatha said, pointing at Coil.

"Y'all got a mess on your hands out there, Sheriff. Be careful and call me if you need anything," Doc said as he shuffled out of the room.

"Well, now I know where Heather's been lately," Agatha said.

"You think he's telling the truth?" Coil asked. "I mean, he did say he had a horsey to catch, and that he was going to have a baby."

"How's Karl been acting lately?"

"Happy, but skittish. Almost scared."

"No doubt. That's what all her exes acted like right before she devoured them. Like a praying mantis."

"Karl doesn't have the kind of checking account that

would appeal to a girl like Heather. What would she want with Karl?" Coil asked.

"Even though that's my best friend you're talking about, I can acknowledge your question has merit. But what she sees in Karl is youth."

Agatha bent over Hank's chest. He'd dropped off to sleep suddenly, but she couldn't even see his chest move. Without opening his eyes, Hank wrapped his left arm around her shoulder and pulled her in for a long, deep kiss. Agatha resisted at first, but Hank's hold held firm.

Hank released her and Agatha could barely catch her breath. "Wow," she said.

"You know I'm not dead, right? I hear everything y'all are saying. I think my funny juice is wearing off. I want more."

"I think you've had your limit, fella," Agatha said, patting his good arm.

"Give him more," Coil said. "I want to know what you did to my pillow while we were roomies at the FBI National Academy."

"I was only kidding."

"I wonder if you were kidding about everything?" Agatha asked.

"I don't recall. What did I say?" Hank asked.

"Okay, you back to being you for a while?" Coil asked, and Hank shot him a thumbs up. "What's this about a horse?"

The medical monitor attached to Hank showed that his pulse and heart rate were climbing again.

"Come on, Hank. You scared of horses or something? Both times they were mentioned, your body went into crazy mode. Just try to calm down."

Hank wormed his big, solid frame up on the inclined

part of the bed. His gown was all but twisted completely off, so he tugged the wafer-thin sheet over his body.

"The horse," he said again.

"And?" Coil asked, exasperated.

"Do you remember the day Aggie and I were outside of Rio Chino to meet the fire marshal? I took that rifle round through the windshield."

"How could I forget?" Agatha asked.

"Don't you remember? There was a guy on a horse riding away."

"Not really. I was in the back seat screaming at you not to ram your car through the fire station door?"

"Oh yeah. But you have to remember me saying something about the horse.

"You know, I do recall that," Coil said. "We were on speaker phone while I radioed Will toward your position."

"And what did Karl see galloping away today?" Hank asked.

"A horse," Agatha and Coil said in unison.

"We need to get the slug from the café floor and compare it to the projectile Will secured from my BMW. I'll bet you anything that they match."

"You think that shot was for me?" Agatha asked.

"Yeah, I do. But just a warning. He wasn't ready to kill you then."

"Which means you think he's ready now," she said. "Lovely."

Hank winced. His brain was still a little sluggish. "If ballistics aren't already in the system with a registered owner, we won't get too far. And why the horse?" Coil asked.

"I've got a good idea who belongs to that rifle, and I've got a theory about the horse. At first I thought it was a practical mode of escaping across a rugged terrain. Now, I've got a symbolic reason, like one of the four horsemen of the apocalypse. I've not weighed it against enough facts just yet."

"Want to clue us in?" Agatha asked, "It is my life after all."

"No. Not yet. I need to let this simmer a bit. You know how loopy my mind is right now." He took her hand in his and then brought it to his lips for a kiss. "You're so beautiful when you laugh."

"Is that you are the meds?" she asked.

"That's my cue to go," Coil said. "I'll give you love birds some privacy. Y'all want coffee or tea?"

"One of each." Agatha said.

"Got it."

Agatha scooted onto the razor-thin edge of the bed. She caressed Hank's left hand. Careful of the IV and electrodes stuck to his body, she wiggled in as close as possible. Hank loved the way she felt next to him, and it showed on the medical monitor.

"Better be careful, or you'll set off a code blue alert," she said, "Can we be serious for a bit?"

"Sure. What's up?" his brow furrowed as he focused on her words.

"I'm serious. What I told you earlier today, not another living soul knows anything about what Salt did to me back then. You, Henry Davidson, are the only person on this planet who knows this. Do you understand how sacred that is to me, and how much I trust you to tell you that?"

"Yes. Yes, I do."

"I was cringing while you were talking out of your head earlier. I just knew after you tattled on Heather and Karl, that you would spill everything I said."

"I said what about Heather and Karl?" He looked surprised.

"That they were having a fling. Don't you remember?" she asked.

"Not really," Hank rubbed at the throb in his temples, "But that was silly stuff. I'd never divulge something that serious."

"Oh, really? You also said you wanted to marry me. Was that just silly stuff?" she asked.

"Oh, yeah," he said, brightening. "That I remember."

Agatha snorted and picked up a bed pillow, holding it over Hank's face while pretending to suffocate him.

"Did I come back at a bad time?" Coil asked.

"Save me," Hank yelled from beneath the pillow. "Or at least give me that coffee."

"Hey, I got this coffee for free with my own good looks. You owe me at least five dollars."

"Free?" Agatha said. "I guess there are perks to being the Sheriff," Agatha joked.

"I ran into Dr. Jacoby down in the lobby. He said the drinks were on him since we'd been working so hard the last couple of days."

Agatha jerked up. "Driscole Jacoby?" she asked.

"Yeah, I think so." Coil smiled as he blew the steam away from the rim of the mug. "Said he drives in two days a week from Austin to do surgeries."

"Don't drink that," she blurted out.

"Why? It's okay. He said it was on him."

"It's Salt," she said, "He's here in the hospital."

Hank threw the pillow on the floor. "How do you figure?"

"Driscole Jacoby was my pharmacology professor at TCU. He used to walk me to the parking lot after night classes. I never told him about Salt, but just that I felt uncomfortable alone walking to my car. He went missing that same semester."

Coil drew his weapon and then pulled a snub nose revolver from the back of his jeans and placed it in Hank's left hand. He hurried to close the thick, wooden door and turned off the lights. He rolled Hank's gurney long ways so it pressed against the door, and he set the brakes on the bed's wheels.

"Agatha, radio Springer and Rodriguez. Make sure they're okay outside and let them know what we got." Coil said.

"Aggie, unplug me," Hank said.

He removed the tape from the IV needle and eased the long, metal spear out of the top of his left hand. He grimaced as he had to move his right arm to get the needle out.

She spoke quietly into the radio. "Springer, this is Agatha, come in."

Nothing.

"Rodriguez, you out there?" she asked.

Nothing.

In the green glow of the medial monitor box, Hank saw Coil press his index finger to his lips to quiet Agatha. Hank motioned for her to come across the room next to him. The one-story hospital also meant they were at ground level with nothing but a glass window between them and whatever was going on outside.

They had all moved away from the door and pressed their backs against the outside wall so that they weren't exposed to the window. The blood rush of activity Hank dizzy and he leaned against Agatha before he collapsed into her and the wall. He felt her trying to support him, but he was just too drained to sit up. He had to catch his breath.

Agatha held up the police radio as it squelched. Hank

peeked out of one eye as if it would help him hear the radio better.

"Hello?" she asked. "Rodriguez? You there?"

The voice that came over the radio sent chills down her spine.

"Class is in session."

Chapter Thirteen

"WE'RE prisoners in our own town," Hank said as his foot connected with the wooden chair in Coil's office.

"You're going to hurt your shoulder if you don't calm down," Agatha said, scolding him.

She was just as upset by the whole episode. They'd been trapped in that tiny hospital room all night. It wasn't until Will and Whitehorse had arrived with reinforcements to search the entire hospital for Salt, that they were rescued. Salt had sedated Coil's deputies and anyone else who had the free coffee and tea in the hospital lobby.

"I can't believe we were that careless. How did he know we were there?" Coil asked.

"I'm begging y'all to understand how dangerous he is. Salt is not some nut job stalker. He's brilliant and deadly. He's going to cat and mouse us until we slip up, and then he'll pick us off. One at a time." She pleaded.

"It ends here," Hank said.

"Let's settle down and think it through. The reality of this is we still don't have evidence of his involvement.

Except for a creepy voice over the radio, we don't even know Salt is here." Coil said.

"I know his voice, Coil. He tormented me with it for over a year. Don't doubt me on this." Agatha's voice was weary. No one had slept in days.

"Guys, can I make a suggestion?" Will spoke quietly.

"Sure," Coil said.

"Why don't we call in the Rangers and FBI? We're tired and injured. It's like Agatha said, he's got us where he wants us."

"I'm not injured," Hank said as he tried to slide his arm out of the cloth sling. He went pale and dropped into the chair closest to him.

Agatha rubbed his left shoulder and slowly set his forearm back in the sling. She was beginning to think they were outmatched, and with the rifle sniper, maybe they were outgunned too.

"This is my town," Coil said. "And I'm not ready to surrender my authority over to a bunch of out-of-towners who care nothing about the damage they do to the people while they're here."

"We're out-of-towners," Whitehorse said.

Coil rolled his eyes. "I didn't mean it like that, Jason."

"I know how you meant it. Just don't let your pride put us in jeopardy."

Agatha walked out of the enclosed room. She felt the tension and knew it would be a matter of how long everyone could keep their cool. No one had slept or rested since Monday, and it showed in the frazzled appearances of hollowed eyes, gaunt cheeks, and deep circles beneath them. She knew they were all moving to a point of mental exhaustion to match their already obvious physical state.

"Okay, I got an idea," Agatha said. "She came back into the office. Let's have a pizza sleep over."

"What?" Will asked.

"We're about to go Breaking Bad on each other. You have to see it coming. Pizza makes everything better, and a nap puts the icing on the cake."

"And where do you suggest we enjoy this childish retreat?" Coil asked.

"I messaged Sheila Johnson, and she said the pizzas will be ready in an hour, and she has enough room at home for everyone to catch shut eye. Springer, Karl, Rodriguez and James are ready to stand guard."

Everyone sat silent and stunned.

She curtsied and said, "You're welcome."

COIL, Hank, Will, Whitehorse and Agatha arrived at Sheila Johnson's house in two vehicles. It was like a covert VIP transport, and Agatha felt like a celebrity, or a high-risk prisoner. Though this was the first time she'd felt safe in the last few days.

"Y'all go in and get relaxed. I'll talk with the team and make sure they don't accept cookies from strangers," Agatha said.

"And no coffee." Coil added.

Whitehorse, who drove the second SUV, jumped out once they arrived at Sheila's. He already had his H&K .9mm submachine gun strapped across his chest. He was ready for battle, or for Salt. He began to scan the area they'd just covered in case there was a tail. The road looked clear. He signaled for the others to go inside.

"Come on in, Jason," Will called from the wide, wrap around wooden porch.

"Y'all enjoy. I'll post up with the deputies."

"You need the rest too."

"I'm okay. We Indians don't get tired. It's in our blood," Whitehorse said, smiling.

"I'll slide a slice of pizza out later."

Agatha waited on the porch with Will just in case he also decided to stand guard. She may not have been a police expert, but she knew pizza and naps were good for the soul. These men all had broken, but good, souls, and she wanted to do what she could to mend them.

"Y'all kick off your shoes and make yourselves at home," Sheila insisted.

Sheila and Hank had become friends. She'd raised Karl alone, and was thankful for the father figure Hank had become in the young man's life. They'd talk at her restaurant at least once a week after she'd lock the place up. They were about the same age, and he enjoyed her friendship. He and Agatha had also learned never to argue with her, so they placed their shoes by the front door.

"I'm so sorry about Penny. I hope y'all catch that no good son…"

"Sheila?" Coil broke off her rant. "I know a good church-going woman like you ain't about to let her tongue fly."

Sheila grinned guiltily. "Sorry, Sheriff. My heart just hurts."

Agatha wrapped her arm around her, "We all do. When are you thinking about reopening the Basket?"

"I don't see how I can. There has been a lifetime of good memories in that place. I started working there for Mr. Mashek before I graduated high school. His family was so good to me. I promised them that if they sold the place to me, that I'd carry on the traditions they'd first started. Death was not one of those traditions."

"I'm so sorry, Sheila," Hank said. He half hugged her with his left arm.

"It's okay, Hammer. Maybe it's time I retired to enjoy those grandbabies Karl is going to give me."

"Grandbabies?" Coil asked.

Agatha stared at him and shook her head no. Sheila strutted around the table straightening the paper plates and napkins. Her smile showed nothing of the reality of closing down the Basket.

"Yep. Seems Karl has found himself a lady friend. They've been regular, so I suspect he'll be making her an honest woman soon. You know I didn't raise that boy to be an ally cat like his daddy. God rest his soul."

"Karl's dad is dead?" Hank asked.

"No," she said. "But I sometimes wish he was." She winked at Hank.

About twenty minutes later, everyone pushed back from the table. The homemade, deep dish pizza was completely gone, except for the slices she'd saved for Whitehorse and the four deputies standing guard.

"Thank you so much," Hank said. "I thought Aggie was nuts when she suggested it this morning, but this is just what we needed."

"You're all so welcome. I've been lonely puttering around this big old house since Monday. I'm thankful to the good Lord that He blessed me with company." She moved gracefully around the table picking up plates and cups.

"I'll bring these plates out to the others," Will said, "I need to walk off some of this food."

"Thanks, Big Willy," Sheila said.

Coil snorted. "Big Willy?"

"I like to give my friends nicknames."

"What's mine?" Coil asked.

"You sure you wanna know, sugar?"

"If he doesn't," Agatha said. "I do."

"He's my Brad Pitt. Cause you fine and you have tight buns."

"That's the best thing I've heard all day," Coil said.

"I could've gone without it," Hank said, grimacing.

"Speaking of good looking," Sheila said. "Who's that deputy? James, I think I know his name, but I don't know his family." Sheila looked out the window.

"That's Jimmie James," Coil said. "He comes from south of Dallas, place called Midlothian. "His claim to fame is that his family is directly descended from Jessie James the outlaw. But he's all lawman, and we're lucky to have him here in Bell County. I suspect he'll be hired by one of the federal agencies soon, unless his relationship to old uncle Jessie gets in the way."

Will walked back into the house.

"Why you holding your boots, Big Willy?" Sheila asked.

"I figure we gotta get going, ma'am."

"Oh, no you don't. Our deal was pizza and a nap. Where I'm from, gentlemen don't eat and run, nor do they sleep with their boots on." She admonished him. "Now, that goes for everyone. You too Mr. Brad Pitt."

"But I have to make a call," Hank said.

"You call later. I've made up enough beds and cots for everyone. The shades are pulled down and it's nice and cozy cool for napping. I'll wake y'all up in thirty minutes."

"What would the boys back at the Rangers say about this, Will?" Coil teased as they moved into the living room.

Will pressed his finger against his lips, "Never say a word."

Agatha, you take this room since the sofa is best for napping. Let the men have the back of the house," Sheila said.

It was easy to see Sheila was in heaven. Agatha agreed

and loved watching the graceful lady enjoy being the perfect hostess. She wondered how many customers Sheila had served in her lifetime. And finally, in her own home, she was again making others comfortable. But they were friends, not customers. Agatha sensed the difference had little effect on Sheila. Her joy came from caring for others.

"You boys go on and get out of here, and let this young lady sleep in peace."

Sheila laughed as she reached up to tug the curtains closed. Agatha watched as she paused to blow her sweet boy, Karl, a kiss, and then tugged a bit more at the heavy, cloth curtains.

Agatha eased onto the couch. It was every bit as comfortable as Sheila said it would be. She adjusted her yoga pants and tugged down on the back of her t-shirt. A few punches to the pillow and it was just right for resting.

"Thanks again, Sheila."

"Thank you, honey, and God bless y'all for taking care of my boy." Sheila turned so she was framed in the window

Agatha closed her eyes and heard the crack of a rifle's report. A burst of red bloomed on Sheila's chest and she looked down in surprise just before she dropped to her knees and crumpled like a rag doll.

Agatha stared in horror with her hands covering her mouth. All she could hear was Karl's screams from outside.

Chapter Fourteen

"You ready to call in the cavalry?" Will asked.

"Let's just stay focused on solving Penny's murder," Coil said.

"And Sheila's." Hank paced the small office.

"Poor Karl." Will said, "That boy will never be the same."

Hank eased into one of the two guest chairs in Coil's office.

"I've got Lieutenant Rodriguez on her way to the regional forensics lab with the bullet fragment we pulled from Sheila's living room wall. We ought to know if it matches the other two soon," Coil said.

Whitehorse poked his head in the office. "Hey, boss, the others are arriving for the briefing."

"How we going to handle this?" Hank asked.

"We're not going to sucker punch Daniel Appleton for sure. I know he'll lead us back to Salt if we allow him a

87

level of comfort. Salt is the skilled one, not that idiot parole officer."

"Right, kill him with kindness," Hank said with a snarl as they walked into the main area.

Hank sat across the room from Appleton. They exchanged glances, and both looked like they'd seen better days. Hank was weary and had an arm in a sling, and Appleton had two black eyes.

"We're going to all head over to Sheila Johnson's home to process the crime scene. The place is secured, and no one has been in since we left a few hours ago. We have a trajectory line from where the rifle was fired, so the FBI's K9 teams can track back that direction in hopes of finding the sniper's nest."

Two FBI special agents dressed in tactical gear and comfortable boots nodded. They were K9 handlers and skilled at tracking. If there was a clue, they'd sniff it out.

"I'd like the detectives from the Rangers' high-crimes to find our suspect, Dr. Ray Salt. He can't be completely off the grid since his release. A credit card, phone call, old family friend. Anything to latch onto him."

"Got it," said a younger female detective with the Texas Rangers. "We're still running track and traces. The guy is a ghost."

Hank saw Appleton's smirk of satisfaction. "Can I also suggest that y'all focus on associations. Very close associations. We understand Salt has a male companion. Seems this special friend is in love with Salt, but Salt thinks of him as a toy." Hank baited the hook.

Appleton's face flushed. His foot began to bob up and down until his knee was shaking the chair. He twisted in his seat toward Hank.

"The Professor is not gay, and neither are any of his companions."

"How would you know, Danny?" Hank pressed.

"My name is not Danny, and I'm his parole officer. I know everything about him and his associates," He said between gritted teeth.

"Then where is Salt?" Hank scowled.

Hank couldn't believe his eyes. There it was. One of the knees on Appleton's khaki pants was stained with mud. Was he that cocky or careless? Either way, the challenge was to get a soil sample from the pants and find the shoot spot on Sheila's property as a comparison. Hank could sense the dragnet was closing in.

"Okay, enough. Everyone has their jobs, let's just do them, alright. These two ladies deserve better than our bickering." Coil scolded the room, but mostly Hank and Appleton.

Hank stormed into Coil's office and slammed the door shut behind him.

"What the heck was that about?" Hank asked Coil.

"Saw what I did?" he asked grinning. "I saw that same patch of grass on his britches, but we need him to stay cool. Remember, friends close—enemies closer."

Hank exhaled. "Sorry. I should've known you saw it too. Let's get going."

"Where's Agatha?" Coil asked.

"She stayed with Karl and Rodriguez. They dropped the bullet fragment off at the lab and then headed over to the coroner's office. Anna is doing the autopsy in Rio Chino, Agatha wanted to keep him company. Plus, we thought it best to get her out of town."

"You think Agatha will punch her?" Coil asked.

Hank grinned. The last time Agatha and Anna Rusk had been in the same room it hadn't ended well. "Will is taking bets. I put five on Agatha."

Coil pursed his lips. "I don't know. Rusk looks tough.

LILIANA HART & LOUIS SCOTT

I'll put five on her." He took money from his wallet and handed it to Coil.

"You realize she'll kill us if she finds out about this," Hank said. "We won't ever see it coming."

"Welcome to the world of relationships," Coil said. "And correction. She'll kill you if she ever finds out. I've got my own wife at home to kill me when I do stupid stuff."

"Yeah, but Shelly's so sweet and gentle."

"Are you drunk? That woman stabbed an outlaw biker in the back a month ago. I've got to sleep with one eye open in my house."

"Good point," Hank said. "You should get a medal."

COIL PULLED his big Dodge Ram pickup truck alongside Deputies Jimmie James and Joe Springer. They were standing guard at the head of Sheila's driveway. There was yellow police tape stretched everywhere and James was recording the names of everyone who entered the crime scene.

The late April afternoon remained cool, so James and Springer didn't seem to mind remaining on watch outside until the others arrived. They were eager to help.

"Hey Springer, would you do me a favor and stick close to that parole officer over there?"

"Sure, Sheriff. Isn't that the one Hank knocked out?"

"Yep."

"Yeah, I don't particularly like him," Springer said.

"Me neither."

All of the officers on scene to help gathered in a common area. The K9 handlers took their dogs from the kennels and let them run around the area on leash. Typical, each dog took turns relieving themselves before it was time to work.

"Appleton, would you take my rookie deputy, Joe Springer with you and cover the K9 teams? He'll appreciate the experience," Coil asked.

"Sure," Appleton agreed.

Hank saw the boastful arrogance on Appleton's face at the idea of showing a rookie the ropes. Appleton had no clue that Springer had better training and instincts than the parole officer would ever have. If there was something suspicious, Springer would sniff it out.

Hank sauntered over to where Appleton was digging in the trunk of his parole officer's vehicle until he found his ballistic vest, helmet and rifle. Hank noticed the rifle was already sitting atop everything else he had in the trunk, and it wasn't secured in the hard plastic carrying case.

"You know, Appleton, I don't like you one bit, but I do respect that you're still here to help," Hank said.

"That's funny, Hank, because I really don't care what you think, or if you like me one bit. I'm assigned here by my boss, and whether I like it or not, I've got a job to finish."

Hank exhaled. He dropped his head, and pretended to be contemplating a snarky reply. In reality, he was taking a detailed visual inventory of Appleton's trunk. Especially his rifle.

The Remington R-25 GII semi-automatic rifle was a .308 Winchester caliber. It was state of the art with its mossy oak camo finish and collapsible synthetic stock. There was no way in the civilized world that the Texas Department of Probation and Parole could afford one, much less hundreds of these specialized rifles for their agents.

Hank also knew it was a hunting or a sniper rifle, and

not something used by an agent in the field to go on raids or make arrests. It was like an elephant gun, and way too much power for hunting mosquitoes.

"Well, that's fair. You might be dim, but at least you're honest," Hank said. chuckling. "Play it straight with our boy here. He's fresh from the academy." Hank patted Springer on the shoulder and slid his sunglasses down to wink at him once he turned away from Appleton.

"Let's get this track going," called out the FBI special agent. "Make sure you two stay back off the dog's trail. He might bite ya."

"He might take a bullet to the snout," whispered Appleton.

Appleton jammed a magazine into his rifle's receiver and slung the big gun around his neck. He slammed his trunk closed and waved for Springer to follow.

Hank walked back to Coil. He was anxious to take the case to the next level, but he wouldn't risk doing a half-way job just because he didn't like Appleton. Time, patience, and evidence would soon sort out the truth.

"Guess what I saw?" Hank pretended to be discussing a tire track.

"I'm sure it's something noteworthy," Coil said out of the side of his mouth.

"Old Danny is packing a high-powered sniper rifle. Winchester .308 caliber. No way it's standard government issue."

"Why would he sling that heavy thing for a K9 track?"

"Because his ego is as big as that bullet. Also, I don't think he knows much about weapons because he missed Agatha twice."

"Yeah, but he hit Sheila once," Coil whispered.

"True. I shouldn't have said that."

"Don't be too hard on yourself. We're close, Hank.

We'll let the detectives see what they can find, and then put more pieces together."

"I know," Hank said. "But it feels like we're wasting our time here. Appleton is only a decoy. Salt is too slick to put himself out, so he's playing puppet master and pulling strings from a safe location."

"I'm curious how Agatha is doing with Karl. That boy is going to need some serious help to get over this. That sure was a bad scene to see."

"I texted Aggie about an hour ago and she said they were all doing okay. Karl is still in shock, but his sense of duty is keeping him from falling apart for now."

"I think after last month, and now this, we're all going to be changed. Maybe we should take a vacation or something. I know Shelly and Cody still haven't slept a full night."

Hank milled around and mostly stayed out of everyone's way. The last thing he wanted to do was wander into anyone's chain-of-custody.

"Will's got something for us," Coil said, waving Hank over.

Hank jogged across the field to where Coil had parked his black Dodge. His chest heaved at the exertion but mostly at being so physically drained over the last week. He read Coil's face.

"Give it to me," he said.

"The bullet fired at y'all in Rio Chino, the bullet fired in the Café, and the bullet that killed Sheila all match," Coil said, reading from a text message Will had sent.

"I knew it," Hank said.

"This is the best part," Coil said, grinning. "It's from a Winchester .308 caliber."

"You're right," Hank said. "That is the best part."

He and Coil leaned against the chrome grill of the

Dodge and waited until they saw Appleton and Springer return. One looked fresh as spring rain, the other was soaking wet with sweat and mud.

"Dang it," Hank said.

"What?"

"I wanted to sample the mud stain on his knee from earlier. Now it's contaminated."

Coil reached into his glove box and handed Hank a brown paper bag. "Like this?"

"No way. How?"

"I'm not above sweeping floors for evidence to convict crooked cops," He said.

Springer hiked over to them. It was easy to see Appleton had tested his patience.

"The guy's a squirrel," Springer said.

"No kidding, but did he teach his rookie anything about police work?" Hank asked.

"Not at all," emphasized Springer. "What's odd though is that weapon. Who carries a half-loaded magazine of .308 rounds?"

"What?" Coil asked.

"Yeah, I saw him stuff a magazine in the rifle before we left. The mag was only half full. It's almost as if he's not even sure how to operate that piece of work."

"You think he'd let you fire it?" Hank came off the truck.

"Where?"

"At that tree, once the others leave."

"He's so desperate to show off in front of me, I bet he would." Springer's eyes were bright with anticipation.

"Y'all hang back and see if he'll let you plant one in that tree. If so, dig it out after he leaves and call me," Coil said.

"No worries. Your rookie is on the case."

Chapter Fifteen

"Whoop," Coil yelled out. They were at their usual table at the Kettle Café.

"Let me guess," Will said. "Springer got the bullet?"

"Yes, sir. Says he'll meet you at the Cracker Barrel to pass off the evidence."

"Amen, that boy deserves a pancake breakfast for pulling that one off." Will dropped a twenty on the table before he headed out to meet Springer.

"So what's the endgame, Coil?" Whitehorse asked.

Coil sipped on his umpteenth cup of coffee and thought through his reply. "If ballistics match, we shock Appleton with an immediate arrest for murder and two counts attempted murder. Then we turn him against Salt. He knows the game. He'll play or he'll rot in prison."

"What if it doesn't match?"

"It will, Jason. It will." Coil crossed his fingers.

Hank kept his head leaned back against the booth and just listened. His mind wandered off to his earlier years on the job. He used to go four or five days without sleep just to snatch a bad guy. Now, he wondered how he did it. His body ached and his head hurt. He'd forgotten about his arm in a sling because the rest of him hurt even more.

"Aggie said they're all on their way back from Rio Chino. Anna did a quick and efficient autopsy. COD was no surprise. Said she'll email a report by morning. Anna told Aggie she had a date and needed to leave on time."

"You okay over that? I know she hurt your feelings."

"Wow, Coil, how about we not over share in mixed company. You know how I felt about that, and it's over now."

Whitehorse wrapped a tattooed, sinewy arm around Hank's shoulder and pretended to smooch at him.

"Did Hanky-Baby get his heart trampled?"

Hank laughed with as much enthusiasm as he could muster.

"Not you too, Whitehorse. I had more respect for you than to do Reggie's bidding."

"Hey, bro, you've grown on me. I hate to see you hurting."

"I'm not hurting. I'm dating Aggie. Who could ask for better?" He grinned mischievously. "I don't mean to rub your noses in it."

"Speaking of robbing the cradle, where are Agatha and my two deputies?" Coil asked.

"On the way back. Said she'd text once they hit the town's limits."

Coil, Whitehorse, and Hank spent the next forty minutes at the café. It made the staff feel better, and they couldn't do anything until the forensics lab results came back. Deputy James was still watching Appleton's every move, and the Ranger's electronic tracking squad had yet to report back a ping on Salt's location.

Hank opened his eyes when he heard and felt Coil's phone dancing on the table's top.

"Shut that thing up, Reggie. I've got a splitting headache," Whitehorse complained.

He could tell by the look on Coil's face it was big. "Tell us what it says."

"We're in business, boys. It's arresting time."

"Let's contact James for a location on Appleton, then get an arrest team over to take him away quietly," Hank suggested.

"Good call. If we don't play this right, Salt will be in the wind and we'll never solve Penny's murder." Whitehorse added.

"Where in the world do you think Salt is, anyway?" Hank pressed his left palm against his throbbing temple."

"Probably right under our noses," Whitehorse said.

It was midnight as they gathered about two miles down the highway from Stanky Thang's Hotel Hideaway. It was a truckers' paradise, and why in the world Appleton would choose this place to stay was beyond Hank's wildest imagination.

"Maybe for the per diem?" James suggested.

"Huh?"

"You know, the state gives you so much per night for a hotel. If you spend less, you keep it. Maybe he needs the cash."

"Okay, well, he'll need bail money soon, so let's get him in custody quick and quiet." Coil said. "Give SWAT the signal. Hank is going with them to make the arrest and begin flipping him."

Whitehorse gave him a thumbs up and radioed to the Texas Rangers' SWAT team and Hank that it was their show.

Hank looked at the tactical unit and signaled it was time to move. He remained safely tucked away at the very end of the stack of officers known as operators. He couldn't move as quickly with his arm still in the sling.

Dressed in all black and armed with heavy weaponry and ballistic vests, helmets and shields, the team moved silently through the night. They had to cross a parking lot full of eighteen wheelers before making it to the double story track of red-brick hotel rooms.

Daniel Appleton was upstairs in room 207. It was located at the east end of the structure. SWAT was aware of his sniper rifle, so they approached from the west side of the hotel. Once they moved around to the stairwell, they picked up steam because the long hallway offered nothing but them as sitting ducks had Appleton opened fire.

The point man on the team held up a heavy bullet-proof shield, while the operator behind him aimed his fully automatic submachine gun to the side of the shield in case Appleton opened the door. Hank waited on the ground floor, but watched as the skill of the SWAT team was obvious.

SWAT slowed as it approached door 207. An operator moved around the one holding the shield. He was completely exposed. He heaved a heavy, solid metal battering ram, called a key, backward, and then let it rip forward as hard and fast as he could propel it.

The door exploded open.

The SWAT team flowed into the room.

The SWAT team quickly exited the room with Appleton in tow.

Hank looked behind the team and back to the room. There might've been a sex care provider peeking through the busted door frame, but Hank figured it was best to leave that part out. Appleton had enough problems.

Coil skidded through the parking lot. Hank pushed Appleton into the back seat of Coil's truck with his left arm, and climbed in behind him. The rear seat area was covered in clear plastic. Hank grinned when Appleton's eyes realized what they were seeing.

"What the he…" Appleton began to scream.

Hank punched him in the mouth with his left hand. It landed solid but wasn't the effect he wanted.

"Screw it," Hank growled as he tugged his right arm out of the sling.

"Listen, you get one chance, and then I turn loose on you. Do you understand me?" Hank asked angrily.

"Do you know who I a…"

Hank punched him in the mouth again. That time he landed a heavy blow with his right fist. It possibly hurt Hank as much as it hurt Appleton.

"One chance." Hank moved within an inch of Appleton's face.

"One chance for what?" he quickly broke and began to weep.

Hank reared his big, hammering fist back. He grimaced in sheer agony, but Appleton wouldn't have known it was pain or hate.

"Okay, please no more. What do you want, a confession?"

"That'll come later."

"Good, I want my lawy…"

Hank smashed his fist harder into Appleton's face. The pain in his shoulder was gone thanks to his spike in adrenaline and the natural endorphins pumping through his body.

"No time for lawyers, Danny. They make clean things, messy. Let's keep this clean, shall we?" Hank's voice dropped an octave deeper and took on a sinister gravel effect.

Hank knew the shifts in his mind and body. It was the darkness that used to be his constant companion. It made violence come easy. It had been in check for a long time now, but the reality of this bum trying to shoot Agatha twice and having just murdered his friend, Sheila, unleashed what he lived to fear most—himself.

"Okay," Appleton begged, "Anything. Yes, let's keep it clean."

"Where is he?"

"Who?"

"Salt." Hank's roar was so loud and vicious that Coil's entire vehicle rattled.

Appleton huddled into a fetal position and sobbed until Hank heard him heaving. There was no mercy. It only further wet Hank's appetite for hurting him.

"Who is Salt?" Appleton offered one last gesture of defiance.

Hank unholstered his .45 caliber pistol, and pressed it into Appleton's mouth. He no longer needed this scum bag, and after hurting people he loved, Hank could only see the red of rage as he cocked the hammer.

"Hank." Coil warned.

"Get out Reggie. This is all on me." He glared at his friend through the rearview mirror.

"Sheriff, don't leave me with him. He'll kill me." Appleton pleaded.

"I'm not going to be a part of this." Coil said, "I've got enough trouble of my own." He opened the driver's door and slipped out.

"Salt," Hank demanded.

"He's right under your nose." Appleton managed to spit the gun's barrel out of his mouth to answer.

"Where?"

"He'll kill me."

"I'll kill you."

Hank shoved the barrel deep into his mouth. He saw chips of teeth cracked against the gun's sight and barrel, but it made no difference to him. Appleton was a killer, and Hank's job was to capture or kill killers.

His hand shook as his right index finger began to tug at the trigger. His shoulder pain may have been masked by the hype, but the strength in his arm and hand was not there.

Appleton blinked his eyelids wildly.

Hank jerked the gun out of his mouth.

"Agatha Harley's home."

Chapter Sixteen

"You sure you're going to be all right, Karl?" Agatha asked. "It's almost one o'clock, why not come back to the office with us?"

"Yes, ma'am. I just need to go lay down and let this soak in," Karl said fighting back tears.

Rodriguez and Agatha watched Karl drag into his apartment, and they drove off once he went inside. Agatha's heart was heavy. She knew what it was to lose her parents. It's something one never really got over.

"Let's head over to the sheriff's office and catch everyone up on what's gone down today," Rodriguez suggested.

"Amen, sister," Agatha said.

"You staying at Hank's again tonight?"

"Yeah, I guess so. We were supposed to head to Fort Worth, but we've been so busy that there's no time to leave."

"No kidding. It's been one heck of a week. Mind if I drop you at the office with someone there and run to my house real quick? It's my daughter's birthday, and I always kiss her at midnight. It's an hour late, but close enough."

"Oh, I'm so sorry you missed it," Agatha said. "Yes, no problem, and if no one is there, I'll lock myself in until they get back."

"Great, thanks so much," Rodrigues said smiling. She had a beautiful smile.

"Could we swing by my place first so I can pick up some fresh clothes? I've been in these same yoga pants all day, and my shirt smells like the morgue. I've got an emergency bag already packed. I just need to grab it."

Rodriguez's lips tightened and she shook her head. "I don't know, Agatha. I'm under strict orders to keep you away from your house."

"Come on," she begged. "Surely you can side with me on this. I need clean clothes and fresh undies."

"Okay, but I'm counting to fifty. If you're not out, I'm coming in to arrest you for trespassing on a crime scene."

"Make it a hundred. I also need makeup."

Rodriguez rolled along Maple Street and passed Hank's home. The outside lights were on, but they knew he wasn't there.

"You're the best bodyguard ever," Agatha said, slamming the car door shut behind her.

Rodriguez rolled down the window. "I'm a cop, not your bodyguard. And I'm counting extra fast."

Agatha sprinted through the yard and onto the porch. The red front door stared at her. She hesitated. It was pitch black. Even the porch lights were off. She swore beneath her breath for having not turned them on the last few days. She fumbled with the door key, and finally wiggled it into the lock to open the door.

It smelled like fingerprint powder. Coil had promised the CSI teams would be extra careful, but investigating crime was a messy business. She moved through the darkened rooms by memory.

Agatha ignored the cold that swept across her body and caused her flesh to pebble. It was the dark and fatigue playing with her mind. She kept telling herself that as she maneuvered into her war room where she kept a go-bag in a built-in bench at the base of her bookshelves.

She grabbed the black nylon bag and slung it over her shoulder. It held a three-day supply of clothes, snacks, and crossword puzzles. Everything a girl would need to survive the apocalypse.

She felt his presence before he spoke.

"Ahh," he said, his words slithering across her skin. "My best student finally came home."

"You shouldn't be here," she said, her voice braver than she felt.

"I've been here all week. It's been nice to live as you've lived. Sleep in your bed. Wash where you shower." He smiled and she saw her death in his eyes. He was crazy, and nothing would satisfy him until he'd taken her life.

"It's stupid for you to be here," she said. "There are cops everywhere. They're always watching."

"I'm not stupid," he said, his voice elevating with anger.

"They'll lock you away again."

He shrugged. "It's not so bad. I'm allowed a lot of… liberties. Besides, they're all busy. They've gone over to arrest that idiot, Appleton."

"There's a cop in the driveway," she said

He laughed, and the sound was like nails on a chalkboard. "Funny, because I think she's leaving. It seems she just got a call that her daughter has been in a terrible accident. Of course, she's still sleeping in her bed, but Officer Rodriguez won't know that until she gets home. It'll be too late for you though."

Agatha peeked out the window to see Rodriguez's patrol car speed away.

"It's just us," Salt said.

"I'm not that same frightened girl anymore, Ray."

"I've told you to call me Dr. Salt," he said angrily. "How many times do I have to tell you?"

Agatha edged over to the side of the chaise. Her fingers trailed along a familiar path. Her daddy's revolver was in the drawer of the end table.

"I'm not afraid of you, Ray."

"Time apart has made you defiant," he said. His breathing was rapid and she could tell he was trying to get it under control.

"I know you're afraid of me, Ray." Using his name was making him angry. And angry people made mistakes. "Why else are you hiding in the dark like a coward?"

"Oh, I'm not hiding. I didn't know you wanted to see me so badly. Here, let me help."

She quietly opened the drawer and reached inside for the gun. She heard the distinctive sound of a lighter and a flame appeared in front of his face. His face glowed orange, but her gaze was caught on the crucifix he held up. The same one that matched the scar on her chest.

"You'll burn for me before it's over," he said, moving closer.

"I don't think so," Agatha said, lifting the revolver. "You'll be too busy burning in hell."

She pulled the trigger, the blast deafening, and she watched in horror as he kept coming. So she kept pulling the trigger until there were nothing but clicks and Salt was face down on the floor.

LILIANA HART & LOUIS SCOTT

"Agatha!" Hank called out. She could hear the sound of footsteps running toward her.

"I'm okay," she called out. "Salt is dead." She was in shock. She knew the signs. It was like she was underwater and everything was in slow motion. And she was so cold.

"Baby," Hank said. "Are you okay?"

"Am I a killer?" she asked, staring up at him as he picked her up in his arms and carried her to the chaise.

"No," he said, kissing her forehead. "You're not a killer. You're free."

"Free," she said, and closed her eyes while the cavalry came.

Epilogue

THE MORNING GLORY Memorial Cemetery was located about three miles outside of town, and the cemetery's manicured lawns were dotted with headstones from as far back as the seventeenth century.

"Karl, your mama was an amazing woman," Agatha said. "And I've got to tell you, she'd have loved this party."

Karl laughed through his tears. He'd decided to honor his mother how she'd have wanted to be remembered. With bright colors and lots of people. And food. More food than anyone could imagine. People from all over Rusty Gun had set up tables and brought pot luck to celebrate at the cemetery.

"You're right about that," he said. "Mama always did like a big gathering. The more the better she said. And if people are going to be standing around, they might as well be eating."

It was a glorious sunny day, and a ray of light beamed down directly on the fresh mound of dirt that covered the casket. Yellow roses covered the top because those were her favorite.

Agatha clung to his arm as they walked away from where they just laid Sheila Johnson to rest. Hank flanked him on the other side.

"Y'all will stay and enjoy the food, won't you?" Karl asked. "I need to go. I just need to…" Emotion clogged his voice and he struggled to find the words. "I just need to be alone for a little while."

"We understand," Agatha said. "Everybody does. Do whatever you have to do. We'll be by to check on you later, and I know Betsy Strobel has set it up so you won't go without a meal for the next year."

"I appreciate everyone," Karl said. "I truly do."

They stopped in front of his unit. He had no other family. No relatives. He was going home to an empty house.

Coil and his wife, and Will and Whitehorse made their way toward them.

Coil put a hand on each of Karl's shoulders and said, "Son, we're your family, and we love you. Tell us when you need us. And tell us when to go away. Sometimes, we might even listen."

Karl cracked a smile. "Yes, sir, Sheriff."

After Karl left, they all decided to go home. The crowd was still heavy at the cemetery, but no one felt much like socializing.

Hank and Agatha went to her Jeep and got inside, buckling up.

"Lord, I'm tired," she said, starting the engine.

"It's not been an easy year. You probably need to take some time for you. You've been through a lot. And there's a lot to process."

"What I'd really like to process is us," she said. "Where do we go from here, Hank?"

She wasn't comforted by the look on his face. He

looked like he was trying to gather his thoughts, and maybe they weren't so good.

"Please, let me say this without stopping," he said. "Or I may not have the courage to try again." His hand covered hers and squeezed gently. "I'm sorry about walking out on you like that. I was hurt, and I don't like being hurt. I guess it means I care if I can be hurt. Does that makes sense?"

She nodded. "Completely."

"I guess I've tried to avoid feeling anything at all since Tammy died. It worked. For the most part. But then I met you, and I couldn't stop feeling things."

"And you felt guilty," she said, understanding.

He nodded, looking at her. "I did. I realized if I was going to truly live again that I had to deal with my past. I started the process back at Christmas, and I can feel the change in me. I'm a work in progress," he said, smiling. "But if you want me to be, I can be *your* work in progress."

Agatha didn't realize she was crying. She threw her arms around him and held him close.

"I don't mind, if you don't mind," she finally said.

He put a finger beneath her chin and lifted it so she was looking him in the eyes. And then he leaned down and kissed her softly.

Sneak Peak - Malice in Wonderland

On Sale - Malice in Wonderland

To Agatha Harley's way of thinking, there were two kinds of rich people in the world. There were those who were comfortable in their wealth, subtle in how they dressed and acted. And there were those who…weren't.

Buck Hazard fit into the latter category. His Dallas ranch was opulent and ostentatious, and Agatha asked herself again how she'd gotten dragged to Buck's annual Fourth of July shindig. She kept coming back to the same answer—*Heather.* Since Heather was one of Buck's ex-wives —his fourth ex-wife to be exact—Agatha figured there was nothing but trouble waiting for them, and she was wound tighter than a drum.

Heather didn't share Agatha's anxiety. She was eating little baby corn in precise rows like it was right off the cob. She kept telling herself there was nothing to feel awkward about. It was totally normal to invite all your ex-wives to the home you'd shared with each of them. Right?

"Stop," Agatha hissed as Heather started in on another

baby corn. "Everyone is looking at you like you just fell off the turnip truck."

Heather snorted. "Darling, they're looking at me because I look every bit like the five million dollars I got in my divorce settlement and they're jealous. These people are all the same. Not a genuine soul in the lot of them."

Agatha looked across the hundreds of people who'd gathered over the green expanse of lawn and around the Olympic-sized swimming pool where the conversation flowed as freely as the margaritas.

"Then I'll ask again," Agatha said. "What in the heck are we doing here?"

"Don't be such a stick in the mud," Heather said. "Have fun. I've counted thirty-two eligible bachelors since we walked through the door, and they all have very nice portfolios. You should try one on for size." Heather waggled her eyebrows.

Agatha didn't figure it was worth asking how Heather knew about their portfolios. When it came to money and men, Heather was better than a crystal ball.

"I'm with Hank," Agatha said. "And these men would bore me to tears. Not an original thought between them. Not to mention the fact that I don't look like a Barbie doll."

The women who were working their charms on the thirty-two eligible bachelors, and some who weren't so eligible, looked like they could've been cut from the same sorority magazine. The dress was anything from star-spangled sequins to barely there bikinis, and Agatha looked down at her own little black dress and cowboy boots and felt even more out of place. She looked like wallpaper standing next to Heather in her electric blue halter dress.

"Honey, you don't marry them for their thoughts. You marry them for the diamonds." Heather shook her head sadly. "I just don't know where I went wrong with you. You'd think I would've rubbed off on you at least a little over the last thirty-something years."

Agatha smiled, feeling herself relax for the first time. "And I love you anyway. Now let's get out of here and drive through Taco Cabana on the way home."

Heather's laugh sounded like a tinkle of bells. "We can't leave yet. Not until I know why Buck wanted me to be here so bad. He said he had something important to tell me."

"What do you think it is?"

"I think he wants me back. I might dangle him along for a little bit, but that ship has sailed, so I'll have to disappoint him."

"I'm sure his current wife will be relieved," Agatha said. "She's the one who's been shooting daggers at you ever since we came through the door."

"A little competition is good for the soul."

"That's a lot of competition," Agatha said. "Buck was married three times before you, and he's been married twice after. They're all here and probably thinking the same thing. I say we get out of here and let them fight over whatever pot Buck is stirring."

"It's not like I'm going to take him back," Heather said. "I just want to play a little and see what he's up to. You know Karl is trying to make an honest woman out of me."

"Does Karl know you're here?"

Heather pouted. "I said he's trying to make an honest woman out of me. Not that he's succeeded. Besides, Buck sounded sad on the phone. Like he needed a friend. And whatever we were, or how we ended up, we were always friends."

A splash and a scream over by the pool had Agatha

jerking around to see what the commotion was all about, but one of the eligible bachelors had jumped in with a bikini-clad woman and she was giving him heck for messing up her hair.

"I'm just saying," Agatha said. "My gut is screaming over this. Stay out of whatever it is he's trying to drag you into."

There was no answer, and when Agatha turned back to where Heather had been standing, there was nothing but an empty margarita glass and half a baby corn on an empty tray.

Agatha sighed and pulled out her phone to send Hank a quick text.

Heather abandoned me. Wish you were here.

It wasn't long before Hank responded. *I miss you like crazy, but you couldn't drag me to that thing in a million years. Hurry back.*

Agatha smiled and went to find Heather. She had a feeling she was with Buck, and Buck should've been easy to find. The man was just past seventy, but he still looked good, probably with the help of a little cosmetic surgery. He looked like an older version of Troy Aikman, and even shared the same height.

Agatha wasn't exactly a shrinking violet. She was close to six-feet in her boots and it was easy to see her over the crowd. She didn't see Heather or Buck, and she let out another sigh just before all heck broke loose.

There was a shrill scream from inside the house that cut through the conversation and Eighties cover band like a knife. Everyone stopped and stared as a streak of electric blue came running out the back door of the house. Agatha shook her head and wondered which of Buck's ex-wives she'd gotten into a fight with. Drama followed Heather around like a dog in heat.

Heather's white blonde hair looked like it had tangled with an egg beater, and she kept screaming as she cut through the crowd like Moses parting the Red Sea. It wasn't until Heather got closer that Agatha could see the genuine fear on her friend's pale face, and she was so distraught she didn't even realize she was heading straight for the pool.

Agatha started in her direction and heard Heather scream out, "He's dead!" just before she tripped into the water.

Enjoy this book? You can make a big difference

Reviews are so important in helping us get the word out about Harley and Davidson Mystery Series. If you've enjoyed this adventure Liliana & I would be so grateful if you would take a few minutes to leave a review (it can be as short as you like) on the book's buy page.

Thanks,

Scott & Liliana

Liliana and I have loved sharing these stories in our Harley & Davidson Mystery Series with you.

There are many more adventures to be had for Aggie and Hank. Make sure you stay up to date with life in Rusty Gun, Texas by signing up for our emails.

Thanks again and please be sure to leave a review where you bought each story and, recommend the series to your friends.

Kindly,
Scott & Liliana

Enjoy this book? You can make a big difference

Reviews are so important in helping us get the word out about Harley and Davidson Mystery Series. If you've enjoyed this adventure Liliana & I would be so grateful if you would take a few minutes to leave a review (it can be as short as you like) on the book's buy page.

Thanks,
Scott & Liliana

Also by Liliana Hart

The MacKenzies of Montana

Dane's Return

Thomas's Vow

Riley's Sanctuary

Cooper's Promise

Grant's Christmas Wish

The MacKenzies Boxset

MacKenzie Security Series

Seduction and Sapphires

Shadows and Silk

Secrets and Satin

Sins and Scarlet Lace

Sizzle

Crave

Trouble Maker

Scorch

MacKenzie Security Omnibus 1

MacKenzie Security Omnibus 2

JJ Graves Mystery Series

Dirty Little Secrets

A Dirty Shame

Dirty Rotten Scoundrel

Down and Dirty

Dirty Deeds

Dirty Laundry

Dirty Money

A Dirty Job

Addison Holmes Mystery Series

Whiskey Rebellion

Whiskey Sour

Whiskey For Breakfast

Whiskey, You're The Devil

Whiskey on the Rocks

Whiskey Tango Foxtrot

Whiskey and Gunpowder

Books by Liliana Hart and Scott Silverii

The Harley and Davidson Mystery Series

The Farmer's Slaughter

A Tisket a Casket

I Saw Mommy Killing Santa Claus

Get Your Murder Running

Deceased and Desist

Malice In Wonderland

Tequila Mockingbird

Gone With the Sin

The Gravediggers

The Darkest Corner

Gone to Dust

Say No More

Lawmen of Surrender (MacKenzies-1001 Dark Nights)

1001 Dark Nights: Captured in Surrender

1001 Dark Nights: The Promise of Surrender

Sweet Surrender

Dawn of Surrender

The MacKenzie World (read in any order)

Trouble Maker

Bullet Proof

Deep Trouble

Delta Rescue

Desire and Ice

Rush

Spies and Stilettos

Wicked Hot

Hot Witness

Avenged

Never Surrender

Stand Alone Titles

Breath of Fire

Kill Shot

Catch Me If You Can

All About Eve

Paradise Disguised

Island Home

The Witching Hour

Also by Louis Scott

Books by Liliana Hart and Louis Scott

The Harley and Davidson Mystery Series

The Farmer's Slaughter

A Tisket a Casket

I Saw Mommy Killing Santa Claus

Get Your Murder Running

Deceased and Desist

Malice in Wonderland

Tequila Mockingbird

Gone With the Sin

Liliana Hart is a New York Times, USAToday, and Publisher's Weekly bestselling author of more than sixty titles. After starting her first novel her freshman year of college, she immediately became addicted to writing and knew she'd found what she was meant to do with her life. She has no idea why she majored in music.

Since publishing in June 2011, Liliana has sold more than six-million books. All three of her series have made multiple appearances on the New York Times list.

Liliana can almost always be found at her computer writing, hauling five kids to various activities, or spending time with her husband. She calls Texas home.

If you enjoyed reading *this*, I would appreciate it if you would help others enjoy this book, too.

Lend it. This e-book is lending-enabled, so please, share it with a friend.

Recommend it. Please help other readers find this book by recommending it to friends, readers' groups and discussion boards.

Review it. Please tell other readers why you liked this

book by reviewing. If you do write a review, please send me an email at lilianahartauthor@gmail.com, or visit me at http://www.lilianahart.com.

Connect with me online:
www.lilianahart.com
lilianahartauthor@gmail.com

facebook.com/LilianaHart

twitter.com/Liliana_Hart

instagram.com/LilianaHart

bookbub.com/authors/liliana-hart

Liliana's writing partner and husband, Scott blends over 25 years of heart-stopping policing Special Operations experience.

From deep in the heart of south Louisiana's Cajun Country, his action-packed writing style is seasoned by the Mardi Gras, hurricanes and crawfish étouffée.

Don't let the easy Creole smile fool you. The author served most of a highly decorated career in SOG buying dope, banging down doors, and busting bad guys.

Bringing characters to life based on those amazing experiences, Scott writes it like he lived it.

Lock and Load – Let's Roll.

Made in the USA
Middletown, DE
24 July 2021